D1048679

Ellen Gilchrist is the author of two novels, *The Annunciation* and *The Anna Papers*; a collection of journals, *Falling Through Space*; and three collections of short stories: *In the Land of Dreamy Dreams*, *Drunk With Love* and *Victory Over Japan*, which won the 1984 American Book Award for fiction. She lives in Fayetteville, Arkansas, USA.

ff

ELLEN GILCHRIST

The Blue-Eyed Buddhist & Other Stories

faber and faber
LONDON · BOSTON

First published in 1990
by Faber and Faber Limited
3 Queen Square, London WC1N 3AU

Photoset by Wilmaset Birkenhead Wirral
Printed in Great Britain by
Richard Clay Ltd Bungay Suffolk

This collection copyright
© Faber and Faber Limited, 1990

'Rich', 'The Famous Poll at Jody's Bar', 'In the Land of Dreamy Dreams' and
'Revenge' first appeared in *In the Land of Dreamy Dreams*,
first published in Great Britain in 1981 by Faber and Faber Limited
© Ellen Gilchrist, 1981

'Victory Over Japan', 'The Gauzy Edge of Paradise', 'The Double Happiness
Bun' and 'Miss Crystal's Maid Name Traceleen, She's Talking, She's Telling
Everything She Knows' first appeared in *Victory Over Japan*, first published in
the USA in 1984 by Little, Brown and Company, Boston, and simultaneously
in Canada
by Little, Brown and Company (Canada) Toronto
First published in Great Britain in 1985 by Faber and Faber Limited
© Ellen Gilchrist, 1983, 1984, 1985

'The Expansion of the Universe', 'Memphis', 'Traceleen at Dawn' and 'The
Blue-Eyed Buddhist' first appeared in *Drunk With Love*, first published in the
USA in 1986 by Little, Brown and Company, Boston, and simultaneously in
Canada
by Little, Brown and Company (Canada) Limited, Toronto
First published in Great Britain in 1987 by Faber and Faber Limited
© Ellen Gilchrist, 1986

The characters and events in these stories are fictitious.
Any similarity to real persons, living or dead, is coincidental
and not intended by the author.

A CIP record for this book is available from the British Library.

ISBN 0-571-15416-6

CONTENTS

RICH

Tom and Letty Wilson were rich in everything. They were rich in friends because Tom was a vice-president of the Whitney Bank of New Orleans and liked doing business with his friends, and because Letty was vice-president of the Junior League of New Orleans and had her picture in *Town and Country* every year at the Symphony Ball.

The Wilsons were rich in knowing exactly who they were because every year from Epiphany to Fat Tuesday they flew the beautiful green and gold and purple flag outside their house that meant that Letty had been queen of the Mardi Gras the year she was a débutante. Not that Letty was foolish enough to take the flag seriously.

Sometimes she was even embarrassed to call the yardman and ask him to come over and bring his high ladder.

'Preacher, can you come around on Tuesday and put up my flag?' she would ask.

'You know I can,' the giant black man would answer. 'I been saving time to put up your flag. I won't forget what a beautiful queen you made that year.'

'Oh, hush, Preacher. I was a skinny little scared girl. It's a wonder I didn't fall off the balcony I was so scared. I'll see you on Monday.' And Letty would think to herself what a big phony Preacher was and wonder when he was going to try to borrow some more money from them.

Tom Wilson considered himself a natural as a banker

1

because he loved to gamble and wheel and deal. From the time he was a boy in a small Baptist town in Tennessee he had loved to play cards and match nickels and lay bets.

In high school he read *The Nashville Banner* avidly and kept an eye out for useful situations such as the lingering and suspenseful illnesses of Pope Pius.

'Let's get up a pool on the day the Pope will die,' he would say to the football team, 'I'll hold the bank.' And because the Pope took a very long time to die with many close calls there were times when Tom was the richest left tackle in Franklin, Tennessee.

Tom had a favourite saying about money. He had read it in the *Reader's Digest* and attributed it to Andrew Carnegie. 'Money,' Tom would say, 'is what you keep score with. Andrew Carnegie.'

Another way Tom made money in high school was performing as an amateur magician at local birthday parties and civic events. He could pull a silver dollar or a Lucky Strike cigarette from an astonished six-year-old's ear or from his own left palm extract a seemingly endless stream of multicoloured silk chiffon or cause an ordinary piece of clothesline to behave like an Indian cobra.

He got interested in magic during a convalescence from German measles in the sixth grade. He sent off for books of magic tricks and practised for hours before his bedroom mirror, his quick clever smile flashing and his long fingers curling and uncurling from the sleeves of a black dinner jacket his mother had bought at a church bazaar and remade to fit him.

Tom's personality was too flamboyant for the conservative Whitney Bank, but he was cheerful and cooperative and when he made a mistake he had the ability to turn it into an anecdote.

'Hey, Fred,' he would call to one of his bosses. 'Come have lunch on me and I'll tell you a good one.'

They would walk down St Charles Avenue to where it crosses Canal and turns into Royal Street as it enters the French Quarter. They would walk into the crowded, humid excitement of the quarter, admiring the girls and watching the Yankee tourists sweat in their absurd spun-glass leisure suits, and turn into the side door of Antoine's or breeze past the maitre d' at Galatoire's or Brennan's.

When a red-faced waiter in funereal black had seated them at a choice table, Tom would loosen his Brooks Brothers' tie, turn his handsome brown eyes on his guest, and begin.

'That bunch of promoters from Dallas talked me into backing an idea to videotape all the historic sights in the quarter and rent the tapes to hotels to show on closed-circuit television. Goddammit, Fred, I could just see those fucking tourists sitting around their hotel rooms on rainy days ordering from room service and taking in the Cabildo and the Presbytere on TV.' Tom laughed delightedly and waved his glass of vermouth at an elegantly dressed couple walking by the table.

'Well, they're barely breaking even on that one, and now they want to buy up a lot of soft porn movies and sell them to motels in Jefferson Parish. What do you think? Can we stay with them for a few more months?'

Then the waiter would bring them cold oysters on the half shell and steaming pompano *en papillote* and a wine steward would serve them a fine Meursault or a Piesporter, and Tom would listen to whatever advice he was given as though it were the most intelligent thing he had ever heard in his life.

Of course he would be thinking, 'You stupid, impotent son of a bitch. You scrawny little frog bastard, I'll buy and sell you before it's over. I've got more brains in my balls than the whole snotty bunch of you.'

'Tom, you always throw me off my diet,' his friend would say, 'damned if you don't.'

'I told Letty the other day,' Tom replied, 'that she could just go right ahead and spend her life worrying about being buried in her wedding dress, but I didn't hustle my way to New Orleans all the way from north Tennessee to eat salads and melba toast. Pass me the French bread.'

Letty fell in love with Tom the first time she laid eyes on him. He came to Tulane on a football scholarship and charmed his way into a fraternity of wealthy New Orleans boys famed for its drunkenness and its wild practical jokes. It was the same old story. Even the second, third, and fourth generation blue bloods of New Orleans need an infusion of new genes now and then.

The afternoon after Tom was initiated he arrived at the fraternity house with two Negro painters and sat in the low-hanging branches of a live oak tree overlooking Henry Clay Avenue directing them in painting an official-looking yellow-and-white-striped pattern on the street in front of the property. 'D-R-U-N-K,' he yelled to his painters, holding on to the enormous limb with one hand and pushing his black hair out of his eyes with the other. 'Paint it to say D-R-U-N-K Z-O-N-E.'

Letty stood near the tree with a group of friends watching him. He was wearing a blue shirt with the sleeves rolled up above his elbows, and a freshman beanie several sizes too small was perched on his head like a tipsy sparrow.

'I'm wearing this goddamn beanie forever,' Tom yelled. 'I'm wearing this beanie until someone brings me a beer,' and Letty took the one she was holding and walked over to the tree and handed it to him.

One day a few weeks later, he commandeered a Bunny Bread truck while it was parked outside the fraternity house making a delivery. He picked up two friends and drove the truck madly around the Irish Channel, throwing fresh loaves of white and whole-wheat and rye bread to the astonished housewives.

'Steal from the rich, give to the poor,' Tom yelled, and his companions gave up trying to reason with him and helped him yell.

'Free bread, free cake,' they yelled, handing out powdered doughnuts and sweet rolls to a gang of kids playing baseball on a weed-covered vacant lot.

They stopped off at Darby's, an Irish bar where Tom made bets on races and football games, and took on some beer and left off some cinnamon rolls.

'Tom, you better go turn that truck in before they catch you,' Darby advised, and Tom's friends agreed, so they drove the truck to the second-precinct police headquarters and turned themselves in. Tom used up half a year's allowance paying the damages, but it made his reputation.

In Tom's last year at Tulane a freshman drowned during a hazing accident at the Southern Yacht Club, and the event frightened Tom. He had never liked the boy and had suspected him of being involved with the queers and nigger lovers who hung around the philosophy department and the school newspaper. The boy had gone to prep school in the East and brought weird-looking girls to rush parties. Tom had resisted the temptation to blackball him as he was well connected in uptown society.

After the accident, Tom spent less time at the fraternity house and more time with Letty, whose plain sweet looks and expensive clothes excited him.

'I can't go in the house without thinking about it,' he said

5

to Letty. 'All we were doing was making them swim from pier to pier carrying martinis. I did it fifteen times the year I pledged.'

'He should have told someone he couldn't swim very well,' Letty answered. 'It was an accident. Everyone knows it was an accident. It wasn't your fault.' And Letty cuddled up close to him on the couch, breathing as softly as a cat.

Tom had long serious talks with Letty's mild, alcoholic father, who held a seat on the New York Stock Exchange, and in the spring of the year Tom and Letty were married in the Cathedral of Saint Paul with twelve bridesmaids, four flower girls, and seven hundred guests. It was pronounced a marriage made in heaven, and Letty's mother ordered masses said in Rome for their happiness.

They flew to New York on the way to Bermuda and spent their wedding night at the Sherry Netherland Hotel on Fifth Avenue. At least half a dozen of Letty's friends had lost their virginity at the same address, but the trip didn't seem prosaic to Letty.

She stayed in the bathroom a long time gazing at her plain face in the oval mirror and tugging at the white lace nightgown from the Lylian Shop, arranging it now to cover, now to reveal her small breasts. She crossed herself in the mirror, suddenly giggled, then walked out into the blue and gold bedroom as though she had been going to bed with men every night of her life. She had been up until three the night before reading a book on sexual intercourse. She offered her small unpainted mouth to Tom. Her pale hair smelled of Shalimar and carnations and candles. Now she was safe. Now life would begin.

'Oh, I love you, I love, I love, I love you,' she whispered over and over. Tom's hands touching her seemed a strange and exciting passage that would carry her simple dreamy existence to a reality she had never encountered. She had never dreamed anyone so interesting would marry her.

Letty's enthusiasm and her frail body excited him, and he made love to her several times before he asked her to remove her gown.

The next day they breakfasted late and walked for a while along the avenue. In the afternoon Tom explained to his wife what her clitoris was and showed her some of the interesting things it was capable of generating, and before the day was out Letty became the first girl in her crowd to break the laws of God and the Napoleonic Code by indulging in oral intercourse.

Fourteen years went by and the Wilsons' luck held. Fourteen years is a long time to stay lucky even for rich people who don't cause trouble for anyone.

Of course, even among the rich there are endless challenges, unyielding limits, rivalry, envy, quirks of fortune. Letty's father grew increasingly incompetent and sold his seat on the exchange, and Letty's irresponsible brothers went to work throwing away the money in Las Vegas and LA and Zurich and Johannesburg and Paris and anywhere they could think of to fly to with their interminable strings of mistresses.

Tom envied them their careless, thoughtless lives and he was annoyed that they controlled their own money while Letty's was tied up in some mysterious trust, but he kept his thoughts to himself as he did his obsessive irritation over his growing obesity.

'Looks like you're putting on a little weight there,' a friend would observe.

'Good, good,' Tom would say, 'makes me look like a man. I got a wife to look at if I want to see someone who's skinny.'

He stayed busy gambling and hunting and fishing and

being the life of the party at the endless round of dinners and cocktail parties and benefits and Mardi Gras functions that consume the lives of the Roman Catholic hierarchy that dominates the life of the city that care forgot.

Letty was preoccupied with the details of their domestic life and her work in the community. She took her committees seriously and actually believed that the work she did made a difference in the lives of other people.

The Wilsons grew rich in houses. They lived in a large Victorian house in the Garden District, and across Lake Pontchartrain they had another Victorian house to stay in on the weekends, with a private beach surrounded by old moss-hung oak trees. Tom bought a duck camp in Plaquemines Parish and kept an apartment in the French Quarter in case one of his business friends fell in love with his secretary and needed someplace to be alone with her. Tom almost never used the apartment himself. He was rich in being satisfied to sleep with his own wife.

The Wilsons were rich in common sense. When five years of a good Catholic marriage went by and Letty inexplicably never became pregnant, they threw away their thermometers and ovulation charts and litmus paper and went down to the Catholic adoption agency and adopted a baby girl with curly black hair and hazel eyes. Everyone declared she looked exactly like Tom. The Wilsons named the little girl Helen and, as the months went by, everyone swore she even walked and talked like Tom.

At about the same time Helen came to be the Wilsons' little girl Tom grew interested in raising Labrador retrievers. He had large wire runs with concrete floors built in the side yard for the dogs to stay in when he wasn't training them on the levee or at the park lagoon. He used all the latest methods for training Labs, including an electric cattle prod given to him by Chalin Perez himself and live ducks supplied by a friend on the Audubon Park Zoo Association Committee.

'Watch this, Helen,' he would call to the little girl in the stroller, 'watch this.' And he would throw a duck into the lagoon with its secondary feathers neatly clipped on the left side and its feet tied loosely together, and one of the Labs would swim out into the water and carry it safely back and lay it at his feet.

As so often happens when childless couples are rich in common sense, before long Letty gave birth to a little boy, and then to twin boys, and finally to another little Wilson girl. The Wilsons became so rich in children the neighbours all lost count.

'Tom', Letty said, curling up close to him in the big walnut bed, 'Tom, I want to talk to you about something important.' The new baby girl was three months old. 'Tom I want to talk to Father Delahoussaye and ask him if we can use some birth control. I think we have all the children we need for now.'

Tom put his arms around her and squeezed her until he wrinkled her new green linen B. H. Wragge, and she screamed for mercy.

'Stop it,' she said, 'be serious. Do you think it's all right to do that?'

Then Tom agreed with her that they had had all the luck with children they needed for the present, and Letty made up her mind to call the cathedral and make an appointment. All her friends were getting dispensations so they would have time to do their work at the Symphony League and the Thrift Shop and the New Orleans Museum Association and the PTAs of the private schools.

All the Wilson children were in good health except Helen. The pediatricians and psychiatrists weren't certain what was wrong with Helen. Helen couldn't concentrate on anything. She didn't like to share and she went through stages of biting other children at the Academy of the Sacred Heart of Jesus.

The doctors decided it was a combination of prenatal brain damage and dyslexia, a complicated learning disability that is a fashionable problem with children in New Orleans.

Letty felt like she spent half her life sitting in offices talking to people about Helen. The office she sat in most often belonged to Dr Zander. She sat there twisting her rings and avoiding looking at the box of Kleenex on Dr Zander's desk. It made her feel like she was sleeping in a dirty bed even to think of plucking a Kleenex from Dr Zander's container and crying in a place where strangers cried. She imagined his chair was filled all day with women weeping over terrible and sordid things like their husbands running off with their secretaries or their children not getting into the right clubs and colleges.

'I don't know what we're going to do with her next,' Letty said. 'If we let them hold her back a grade it's just going to make her more self-conscious than ever.'

'I wish we knew about her genetic background. You people have pull with the sisters. Can't you find out?'

'Tom doesn't want to find out. He says we'll just be opening a can of worms. He gets embarrassed even talking about Helen's problem.'

'Well,' said Dr Zander, crossing his short legs and settling his steel-rimmed glasses on his nose like a tiny bicycle stuck on a hill, 'let's start her on Dexedrine.'

So Letty and Dr Zander and Dr Mullins and Dr Pickett and Dr Smith decided to try an experiment. They decided to give Helen five milligrams of Dexedrine every day for twenty days each month, taking her off the drug for ten days in between.

'Children with dyslexia react to drugs strangely,' Dr Zander said. 'If you give them tranquillizers it peps them up, but if you give them Ritalin or Dexedrine it calms them down and makes them able to think straight.'

'You may have to keep her home and have her tutored on the days she is off the drug,' he continued, 'but the rest of the time she should be easier to live with.' And he reached over and patted Letty on the leg and for a moment she thought it might all turn out all right after all.

Helen stood by herself on the playground of the beautiful old pink-brick convent with its drooping wrought-iron balconies covered with ficus. She was watching the girl she liked talking with some other girls who were playing jacks. All the girls wore blue-and-red-plaid skirts and navy blazers or sweaters. They looked like a disorderly marching band. Helen was waiting for the girl, whose name was Lisa, to decide if she wanted to go home with her after school and spend the afternoon. Lisa's mother was divorced and worked downtown in a department store, so Lisa rode the streetcar back and forth from school and could go anywhere she liked until five-thirty in the afternoon. Sometimes she went home with Helen so she wouldn't have to ride the streetcar. Then Helen would be so excited the hours until school let out would seem to last forever.

Sometimes Lisa liked her and wanted to go home with her and other times she didn't, but she was always nice to Helen and let her stand next to her in lines.

Helen watched Lisa walking toward her. Lisa's skirt was two inches shorter than those of any of the other girls, and she wore high white socks that made her look like a skater. She wore a silver identification bracelet and Revlon nail polish.

'I'll go home with you if you get your mother to take us to get an Icee,' Lisa said. 'I was going last night but my mother's boyfriend didn't show up until after the place closed so I was going to walk to Manny's after school. Is that OK?'

'I think she will,' Helen said, her eyes shining. 'I'll go call her up and see.'

'Naw, let's just go swing. We can ask her when she comes.' Then Helen walked with her friend over to the swings and tried to be patient waiting for her turn.

The Dexedrine helped Helen concentrate and it helped her get along better with other people, but it seemed to have an unusual side effect. Helen was chubby and Dr Zander had led the Wilsons to believe the drug would help her lose weight, but instead she grew even fatter. The Wilsons were afraid to force her to stop eating for fear they would make her nervous, so they tried to reason with her.

'Why can't I have any ice cream?' she would say. 'Daddy is fat and he eats all the ice cream he wants.' She was leaning up against Letty, stroking her arm and petting the baby with her other hand. They were in an upstairs sitting room with the afternoon sun streaming in through the French windows. Everything in the room was decorated with different shades of blue, and the curtains were white with old-fashioned blue-and-white-checked ruffles.

'You can have ice cream this evening after dinner,' Letty said, 'I just want you to wait a few hours before you have it. Won't you do that for me?'

'Can I hold the baby for a while?' Helen asked, and Letty allowed her to sit in the rocker and hold the baby and rock it furiously back and forth crooning to it.

'Is Jennifer beautiful, Mother?' Helen asked.

'She's OK, but she doesn't have curly black hair like you. She just has plain brown hair. Don't you see, Helen, that's why we want you to stop eating between meals, because you're so pretty and we don't want you to get too fat. Why don't you go outside and play with Tim and not try to think about ice cream so much?'

'I don't care,' Helen said, 'I'm only nine years old and I'm hungry. I want you to tell the maids to give me some ice cream now,' and she handed the baby to her mother and ran out of the room.

The Wilsons were rich in maids, and that was a good thing because there were all those children to be taken care of and cooked for and cleaned up after. The maids didn't mind taking care of the Wilson children all day. The Wilsons' house was much more comfortable than the ones they lived in, and no one cared whether they worked very hard or not as long as they showed up on time so Letty could get to her meetings. The maids left their own children with relatives or at home watching television, and when they went home at night they liked them much better than if they had spent the whole day with them.

The Wilson house had a wide white porch across the front and down both sides. It was shaded by enormous oak trees and furnished with swings and wicker rockers. In the afternoons the maids would sit on the porch and other maids from around the neighbourhood would come up pushing prams and strollers and the children would all play together on the porch and in the yard. Sometimes the maids fixed lemonade and the children would sell it to passersby from a little stand.

The maids hated Helen. They didn't care whether she had dyslexia or not. All they knew was that she was a lot of trouble to take care of. One minute she would be as sweet as pie and cuddle up to them and say she loved them and the next minute she wouldn't do anything they told her.

'You're a nigger, nigger, nigger, and my mother said I could cross St Charles Avenue if I wanted to,' Helen would say, and the maids would hold their lips together and look into each other's eyes.

One afternoon the Wilson children and their maids were sitting on the porch after school with some of the neighbours' children and maids. The baby was on the porch in a bassinet on wheels and a new maid was looking out for her. Helen was in the biggest swing and was swinging as high as she could go so that none of the other children could get in the swing with her.

'Helen,' the new maid said, 'it's Tim's turn in the swing. You been swinging for fifteen minutes while Tim's been waiting. You be a good girl now and let Tim have a turn. You too big to act like that.'

'You're just a high yeller nigger,' Helen called, 'and you can't make me do anything.' And she swung up higher and higher.

This maid had never had Helen call her names before and she had a quick temper and didn't put up with children calling her a nigger. She walked over to the swing and grabbed the chain and stopped it from moving.

'You say you're sorry for that, little fat honky white girl,' she said, and made as if to grab Helen by the arms, but Helen got away and started running, calling over her shoulder, 'nigger, can't make me do anything.'

She was running and looking over her shoulder and she hit the bassinet and it went rolling down the brick stairs so fast none of the maids or children could stop it. It rolled down the stairs and threw the baby onto the sidewalk and the blood from the baby's head began to move all over the concrete like a little ruby lake.

The Wilsons' house was on Philip Street, a street so rich it even had its own drugstore. Not some tacky chain drugstore with everything on special all the time, but a cute drugstore made out of a frame bungalow with gingerbread trim. Every-thing inside cost twice as much as it did in a regular drugstore, and the grown people could order any kind of drugs they needed and a green Mazda pickup would bring them right over. The children had to get their drugs from a fourteen-year-old pusher in Audubon Park named Leroi, but they could get all the ice cream and candy and chewing gum they wanted from the drugstore and charge it to their parents.

No white adults were at home in the houses where the maids worked so they sent the children running to the drugstore to bring the druggist to help with the baby. They called the hospital and ordered an ambulance and they called several doctors and they called Tom's bank. All the children who were old enough ran to the drugstore except Helen. Helen sat on the porch steps staring down at the baby with the maids hovering over it like swans, and she was crying and screaming and beating her hands against her head. She was in one of the periods when she couldn't have Dexedrine. She screamed and screamed, but none of the maids had time to help her. They were too busy with the baby.

'Shut up, Helen,' one of the maids called. 'Shut up that goddamn screaming. This baby is about to die.'

A police car and the local patrol service drove up. An ambulance arrived and the yard filled with people. The druggist and one of the maids rode off in the ambulance with the baby. The crowd in the yard swarmed and milled and swam before Helen's eyes like a parade.

Finally they stopped looking like people and just looked like spots of colour on the yard. Helen ran up the stairs and climbed under her cherry four-poster bed and pulled her pillows and her eiderdown comforter under it with her. There were cereal boxes and an empty ice cream carton and half a tin of English cookies under the headboard. Helen was soaked with sweat and her little Lily playsuit was tight under her arms and cut into her flesh. Helen rolled up in the comforter and began to dream the dream of the heavy clouds. She dreamed she was praying, but the beads of the rosary slipped through her fingers so quickly she couldn't catch them and it was cold in the church and beautiful and fragrant, then dark, then light, and Helen was rolling in the heavy clouds that rolled her like biscuit dough. Just as she was about to suffocate they rolled her face up to the blue air above the clouds. Then Helen was a pink kite floating above the houses at evening. In the yards children were playing and fathers were driving up and baseball games were beginning and the sky turned grey and closed upon the city like a lid.

And now the baby is alone with Helen in her room and the door is locked and Helen ties the baby to the table so it won't fall off.

'Hold still, Baby, this will just be a little shot. This won't hurt much. This won't take a minute.' And the baby is still and Helen begins to work on it.

Letty knelt down beside the bed. 'Helen, please come out from under there. No one is mad at you. Please come out and help me, Helen. I need you to help me.'

Helen held on tighter to the slats of the bed and squeezed her eyes shut and refused to look at Letty.

Letty climbed under the bed to touch the child. Letty was crying and her heart had an anchor in it that kept digging in and sinking deeper and deeper.

Dr Zander came into the bedroom and knelt beside the bed and began to talk to Helen. Finally he gave up being reasonable and wiggled his small grey-suited body under the bed and Helen was lost in the area of arms that tried to hold her.

*

Tom was sitting in the bank president's office trying not to let Mr Saunders know how much he despised him or how much it hurt and mattered to him to be listening to a lecture. Tom thought he was too old to have to listen to lectures. He was tired and he wanted a drink and he wanted to punch the bastard in the face.

'I know, I know,' he answered, 'I can take care of it. Just give me a month or two. You're right. I'll take care of it.'

And he smoothed the pants of his cord suit and waited for the rest of the lecture.

A man came into the room without knocking. Tom's secretary was behind him.

'Tom, I think your baby has had an accident. I don't know any details. Look, I've called for a car. Let me go with you.'

Tom ran up the steps of his house and into the hallway full of neighbours and relatives. A girl in a tennis dress touched him on the arm, someone handed him a drink. He ran up the winding stairs to Helen's room. He stood in the doorway. He could see Letty's shoes sticking out from under the bed. He could hear Dr Zander talking. He couldn't go near them.

'Letty,' he called, 'Letty, come here, my god, come out from there.'

No one came to the funeral but the family. Letty wore a plain dress she would wear any day and the children all wore their school clothes.

The funeral was terrible for the Wilsons, but afterward they went home and all the people from the Garden District and from all over town started coming over to cheer them up. It looked like the biggest cocktail party ever held in New Orleans. It took four rented butlers just to serve the drinks. Everyone wanted to get in on the Wilson's tragedy.

*

In the months that followed the funeral Tom began to have sinus headaches for the first time in years. He was drinking a lot and smoking again. He was allergic to whisky, and when he woke up in the morning his nose and head were so full of phlegm he had to vomit before he could think straight.

He began to have trouble with his vision.

One November day the high yellow windows of the Shell Oil Building all turned their eyes upon him as he stopped at the corner of Poydras and Carondelet to wait for a street-light, and he had to pull the car over to the curb and talk to himself for several minutes before he could drive on.

He got back all the keys to his apartment so he could go there and be alone and think. One afternoon he left work at two o'clock and drove around Jefferson Parish all afternoon drinking Scotch and eating potato chips.

Not as many people at the bank wanted to go out to lunch with him anymore. They were sick and tired of pretending his expensive mistakes were jokes.

One night Tom was gambling at the Pickwick Club with a poker group and a man jokingly accused him of cheating. Tom jumped up from the table, grabbed the man and began hitting him with his fists. He hit the man in the mouth and knocked out his new gold inlays.

'You dirty little goddamn bond peddler, you son of a bitch! I'll kill you for that,' Tom yelled, and it took four waiters to hold him while the terrified man made his escape. The next morning Tom resigned from the club.

He started riding the streetcar downtown to work so he wouldn't have to worry about driving his car home if he got drunk. He was worrying about money and he was worrying about his gambling debts, but most of the time he was thinking about Helen. She looked so much like him that he believed people would think she was his illegitimate child.

The more he tried to talk himself into believing the baby's death was an accident, the more obstinate his mind became.

The Wilson children were forbidden to take the Labs out of the kennels without permission. One afternoon Tom came home earlier than usual and found Helen sitting in the open door of one of the kennels playing with a half-grown litter of puppies. She was holding one of the puppies and the others were climbing all around her and spilling out onto the grass. She held the puppy by its forelegs, making it dance in the air, then letting it drop. Then she would gather it in her arms and hold it tight and sing to it.

Tom walked over to the kennel and grabbed her by an arm and began to paddle her as hard as he could.

'Goddamn you, what are you trying to do? You know you aren't supposed to touch those dogs. What in the hell do you think you're doing?'

Helen was too terrified to scream. The Wilsons never spanked their children for anything.

'I didn't do anything to it. I was playing with it,' she sobbed.

Letty and the twins came running out of the house and when Tom saw Letty he stopped hitting Helen and walked in through the kitchen door and up the stairs to the bedroom. Letty gave the children to the cook and followed him.

Tom stood by the bedroom window trying to think of something to say to Letty. He kept his back turned to her and he was making a nickel disappear with his left hand. He thought of himself at Tommie Keenen's birthday party wearing his black coat and hat and doing his famous rope trick. Mr Keenen had given him fifteen dollars. He remembered sticking the money in his billfold.

'My God, Letty, I'm sorry. I don't know what the shit's going on. I thought she was hurting the dog. I know I shouldn't have hit her and there's something I need to tell you about the bank. Kennington is getting sacked. I may be part of the housecleaning.'

'Why didn't you tell me before? Can't Daddy do anything?'

'I don't want him to do anything. Even if it happens it doesn't have anything to do with me. It's just bank politics. We'll say I quit. I want to get out of there anyway. That fucking place is driving me crazy.'

Tom put the nickel in his pocket and closed the bedroom door. He could hear the maid down the hall comforting Helen. He didn't give a fuck if she cried all night. He walked over to Letty and put his arms around her. He smelled like he'd been drinking for a week. He reached under her dress and pulled down her pantyhose and her underpants and began kissing her face and hair while she stood awkwardly with the pants and hose around her feet like a halter. She was trying to cooperate.

She forgot that Tom smelled like sweat and whisky. She was thinking about the night they were married. Every time they made love Letty pretended it was that night. She had spent thousands of nights in a bridal suite at the Sherry Netherland Hotel in New York City.

Letty lay on the walnut bed leaning into a pile of satin pillows and twisting a gold bracelet around her wrist. She could hear the children playing outside. She had a headache and her stomach was queasy, but she was afraid to take a Valium or an aspirin. She was waiting for the doctor to call her back and tell her if she was pregnant. She already knew what he was going to say.

Tom came into the room and sat by her on the bed.

'What's wrong?'

'Nothing's wrong. Please don't do that. I'm tired.'

'Something's wrong.'

'Nothing's wrong. Tom, please leave me alone.'

Tom walked out through the French windows and on to a little balcony that overlooked the play yard and the dog runs. Sunshine flooded Philip Street, covering the houses and trees and dogs and children with a million volts a minute. It flowed down to hide in the roots of trees, glistening on the cars, baking the street, and lighting Helen's rumpled hair where she stooped over the puppy. She was singing a little song. She had made up the song she was singing.

'The baby's dead. The baby's dead. The baby's gone to heaven.'

'Jesus God,' Tom muttered. All up and down Philip Street fathers were returning home from work. A jeep filled with teenagers came tearing past and threw a beer can against the curb.

Six or seven pieces of Tom's mind sailed out across the street and stationed themselves along the power line that zigzagged back and forth along Philip Street between the live oak trees.

The pieces of his mind sat upon the power line like a row of black starlings. They looked him over.

Helen took the dog out of the buggy and dragged it over to the kennel.

'Jesus Christ,' Tom said, and the pieces of his mind flew back to him as swiftly as they had flown away and entered his eyes and ears and nostrils and arranged themselves in their proper places like parts of a phrenological head.

Tom looked at his watch. It said 6.15. He stepped back into the bedroom and closed the French windows. A vase of huge roses from the garden hid Letty's reflection in the mirror.

'I'm going to the camp for the night. I need to get away. Besides, the season's almost over.'

'All right,' Letty answered. 'Who are you going with?'

'I think I'll take Helen with me. I haven't paid any attention to her for weeks.'

'That's good,' Letty said, 'I really think I'm getting a cold. I'll have a tray up for supper and try to get some sleep.'

Tom moved around the room, opening drawers and closets and throwing some gear into a canvas duffel bag. He changed into his hunting clothes.

He removed the guns he needed from a shelf in the upstairs den and cleaned them neatly and thoroughly and zipped them into their carriers.

'Helen,' he called from the downstairs porch, 'Bring the dog in the house and come get on some play clothes. I'm going to take you to the duck camp with me. You can take the dog.'

'Can we stop and get beignets?' Helen called back, coming running at the invitation.

'Sure we can, honey. Whatever you like. Go get packed. We'll leave as soon as dinner is over.'

It was nine o'clock at night. They crossed the Mississippi River from the New Orleans side on the last ferry going to Algier's Point. There was an offshore breeze and a light rain fell on the old brown river. The Mississippi River smelled like the inside of a nigger cabin, powerful and fecund. The smell came in Tom's mouth until he felt he could chew it.

He leaned over the railing and vomited. He felt better and walked back to the red Chevrolet pickup he had given himself for a birthday present. He thought it was chic for a banker to own a pickup.

Helen was playing with the dog, pushing him off the seat and laughing when he climbed back on her lap. She had a paper bag of doughnuts from the French Market and was eating them and licking the powdered sugar from her fingers and knocking the dog off the seat.

She wasn't the least bit sleepy.

'I'm glad Tim didn't get to go. Tim was bad at school, that's why he had to stay home, isn't it? The sisters called Momma. I don't like Tim. I'm glad I got to go by myself.' She stuck her fat arms out the window and rubbed Tom's canvas hunting jacket. 'This coat feels hard. It's all dirty. Can we go up in the cabin and talk to the pilot?'

'Sit still, Helen.'

'Put the dog in the back, he's bothering me.' She bounced up and down on the seat. 'We're going to the duck camp. We're going to the duck camp.'

The ferry docked. Tom drove the pickup onto the blacktop road past the city dump and on into Plaquemines Parish.

They drove into the brackish marshes that fringe the Gulf of Mexico where it extends in ragged fingers along the coast below and to the east of New Orleans. As they drove closer to the sea the hardwoods turned to palmetto and water oak and willow.

The marshes were silent. Tom could smell the glasswort and black mangrove, the oyster and shrimp boats.

He wondered if it were true that children and dogs could penetrate a man's concealment, could know him utterly.

Helen leaned against his coat and prattled on.

In the Wilson house on Philip Street Tim and the twins were cuddled up by Letty, hearing one last story before they went to bed.

A blue wicker tray held the remains of the children's hot chocolate. The china cups were a confirmation present sent to Letty from Limoges, France.

Now she was finishing reading a wonderful story by Ludwig Bemelmans about a little convent girl in Paris named Madeline who reforms the son of the Spanish ambassador, putting an end to his terrible habit of beheading chickens on the miniature guillotine.

Letty was feeling better. She had decided God was just trying to make up to her for Jennifer.

The camp was a three-room wooden shack built on pilings out over Bayou Lafouche, which runs through the middle of the parish.

The inside of the camp was casually furnished with old leather office furniture, hand-me-down tables and lamps, and a walnut poker table from Neiman-Marcus. Photographs of hunts and parties were tacked around the walls. Over the poker table were pictures of racehorses and their owners and an assortment of ribbons won in races.

Tom laid the guns down on the bar and opened a cabinet over the sink in the part of the room that served as a kitchen. The nigger hadn't come to clean up after the last party and the sink was piled with half-washed dishes. He found a clean glass and a bottle of Tanqueray gin and sat down behind the bar.

Helen was across the room on the floor finishing the beignets and trying to coax the dog to come closer. He was considering it. No one had remembered to feed him.

Tom pulled a new deck of cards out of a drawer, broke the seal, and began to shuffle them.

Helen came and stood by the bar. 'Show me a trick Daddy. Make the queen disappear. Show me how to do it.'

'Do you promise not to tell anyone the secret? A magician never tells his secrets.'

'I won't tell. Daddy, please show me, show me now.'

Tom spread out the cards. He began to explain the trick.

'All right, you go here and here, then here. Then pick up

these in just the right order, but look at the people while you do it, not at the cards.'

'I'm going to do it for Lisa.'

'She's going to beg you to tell the secret. What will you do then?'

'I'll tell her a magician never tells his secrets.'

Tom drank the gin and poured some more.

'Now let me do it to you, Daddy.'

'Not yet, Helen. Go sit over there with the dog and practice it where I can't see what you're doing. I'll pretend I'm Lisa and don't know what's going on.'

Tom picked up the Kliengunther 7 mm magnum rifle and shot the dog first, splattering its brains all over the door and walls. Without pausing, without giving her time to raise her eyes from the red and grey and black rainbow of the dog, he shot the little girl.

The bullet entered her head from the back. Her thick body rolled across the hardwood floor and lodged against a hat rack from Jody Mellon's old office in the Hibernia Bank Building. One of her arms landed on a pile of old *Penthouse* magazines and her disordered brain flung its roses north and east and south and west and rejoined the order from which it casually arose.

Tom put down the rifle, took a drink of the thick gin, and, carrying the pistol, walked out onto the pier through the kitchen door. Without removing his glasses or his hunting cap he stuck the .38 Smith and Wesson revolver against his palate and splattered his own head all over the new pier and the canvas covering of the Boston Whaler. His body struck the boat going down and landed in eight feet of water beside a broken crab trap left over from the summer.

A pair of deputies from the Plaquemines Parish sheriff's office found the bodies.

Everyone believed it was some terrible inexplicable mistake or accident.

No one believed that much bad luck could happen to a nice lady like Letty Dufrechou Wilson, who never hurt a flea or gave anyone a minute's trouble in her life.

No one believed that much bad luck could get together between the fifteenth week after Pentecost and the third week in Advent.

No one believed a man would kill his own little illegitimate dyslexic daughter just because she was crazy.

And no one, not even the district attorney of New Orleans, wanted to believe a man would shoot a $3,000 Labrador retriever sired by Super Chief out of Prestidigitation.

THE FAMOUS POLL AT JODY'S BAR

It was ninety-eight degrees in the shade in New Orleans, a record-breaking day in August.

Nora Jane Whittington sat in a small apartment several blocks from Jody's Bar and went over her alternatives.

'No two ways about it,' she said to herself, shaking out her black curls, 'if Sandy wants my ass in San José, I'm taking it to San José. But I've got to get some cash.'

Nora Jane was nineteen years old, a self-taught anarchist and a quick-change artist. She owned six Dynel wigs in different hair colours, a makeup kit she stole from Le Petit Theatre du Vieux Carre while working as a volunteer stage-hand, and a small but versatile wardrobe. She could turn her graceful body into any character she saw in a movie or on TV. Her specialties were boyish young lesbians, boyish young nuns, and a variety of lady tourists.

Nora Jane could also do wonderful tricks with her voice, which had a range of almost two octaves. She was the despair of the sisters at the Academy of the Most Holy Name of Jesus when she quit the choir saying her chores at home didn't allow her to stay after school to practise.

The sisters made special novenas for the bright, lonely child whose father died at the beginning of the Vietnam War and whose pretty alcoholic mother wept and prayed when they called upon her begging her to either put away the bottle and make a decent home for Nora Jane or allow them to put her in a Catholic boarding school.

Nora Jane didn't want a decent home. What she wanted was a steady boyfriend, and the summer she graduated from high school she met Sandy. Nora Jane had a job selling records at The Mushroom Cloud, a record shop near the Tulane campus where rich kids came to spend their parents' money on phonograph records and jewellery made in the shape of coke spoons and marijuana leaves. 'The Cloud' was a nice place, up a flight of narrow stairs from Freret Street. Nora Jane felt important, helping customers decide what records to buy.

The day Sandy came into her life she was wearing a yellow cotton dress and her hair was curling around her face from the humidity.

Sandy walked into the shop and stood for a long time reading the backs of jazz albums. He was fresh out of a Texas reform school with $500 in the bank and a new lease on life. He was a handsome boy with green eyes as opaque and unfathomable as a salt lake. When he smiled down at Nora Jane over a picture of Rahshaan Roland Kirk as The Five Thousand Pound Man, she dreamed of Robert Redford as The Sundance Kid.

'I'm going to dedicate a book of poems to this man's memory,' Sandy said. 'I'm going to call the book *Dark Mondays*. Did you know that Rahshaan Kirk died last year?'

'I don't know much about him. I haven't been working here long,' Nora Jane said. 'Are you really a writer?'

'I'm really a land surveyor, but I write poems and stories at night. In the school I went to in Texas a poet used to come and teach my English class once a month. He said the most important writing gets done in your head while you think you're doing something else. Sometimes I write in the fields while I'm working. I sing the poems I'm writing to myself like work songs. Then at night I write them down. You really ought to listen to this album. Rahshaan Kirk is almost as good as Coltrane. A boy I went to school with his cousin.'

'I guess I have a lot to learn about different kinds of music,' Nora Jane answered, embarrassed.

'I'm new in town,' Sandy said, after they had talked for a while, 'and I don't know many people here yet. How about going with me to a political rally this afternoon. I read in the paper that The Alliance for Good Government is having a free picnic in Audubon Park. I like to find out what's going on in politics when I get to a new town.'

'I don't know if I should,' Nora Jane said, trying not to smile.

'It's all right,' Sandy told her. 'I'm really a nice guy. You'll be safe with me. It isn't far from here and we have to walk anyway because I don't have a car, so if you don't like it you can just walk away. If you'll go I'll wait for you after work.'

'I guess I should go,' Nora Jane said. 'I need to know what's going on in politics myself.'

When Nora Jane was through for the day they walked to Audubon Park and ate free fried chicken and listened to the Democratic candidate for the House of Representatives debate the Republican candidate over the ERA and the canal treaties.

It was still light when they walked back through the park in the direction of Sandy's apartment. Nora Jane was telling Sandy the story of her life. She had just gotten to the sad part where her father died when he stopped her and put his hands around her waist.

'Wait just a minute,' he said, and he walked over to the roots of an enormous old live-oak tree and began to dig a hole with the heel of his boot. When he had dug down about six inches in the hard-packed brown soil he took out all the change he had in his pockets, wrapped it in a dollar bill and buried it in the hole. He packed the dirt back down with his hands and looked up at her.

'Remember this spot,' he said, 'you might need this some day.'

Many hours later Nora Jane reached out and touched his arm where he stood leaning into the window frame watching the moon in the cloudy sky.

'Do you want to stay here for a while?' he asked, without looking at her.

'I want to stay here for a long time,' she answered, taking a chance.

So she stayed for fourteen months.

Sandy taught her how to listen to jazz, how to bring a kite down without tearing it, how to watch the sun go down on the Mississippi River, how to make macrame plant holders out of kite string, and how to steal things.

Stealing small things from elegant uptown gift shops was as easy as walking down a tree-lined street. After all, Sandy assured her, their insurance was covering it. Pulling off robberies was another thing. Nora Jane drove the borrowed getaway car three times while Sandy cleaned out a drugstore and two beauty parlours in remote parts of Jefferson Parish. The last of these jobs supplied her with the wigs. Sandy picked them up for her on his way out.

'I'm heading for the west coast,' he told her, when the beauty parlour job turned out to be successful beyond his wildest dreams, netting them $723. He had lucked into a payroll.

'I'll send for you as soon as I get settled,' he said, and he lifted her over his head like a flower and carried her to the small iron bed and made love to her while the afternoon sun and then the moonlight poured in the low windows of the attic apartment.

Robbing a neighbourhood bar in uptown New Orleans in broad daylight all by herself was another thing entirely. Nora Jane thought that up for herself. It was the plan she settled upon as the quickest way to get to California. She planned it for weeks, casing the bar at different times of the day and night in several disguises, and even dropping by one Saturday afternoon pretending to be collecting money to help the Crippled Children's Hospital. She collected almost ten dollars.

Nora Jane had never been out of the state of Louisiana, but once she settled on a plan of action she was certain all she needed was a little luck and she was as good as wading in the Pacific Ocean. One evening's work and her hands were back in Sandy's hair.

She crossed herself and prayed for divine intervention. After all, she told herself, robbing an old guy who sold whisky and laid bets on athletic events was part of an anarchist's work. Nora Jane didn't like old guys much anyway. They were all wrinkled where the muscles ought to be and they were so sad.

She took the heavy stage pistol out of its hiding place under the sink and inspected it. She practised looking tough for a few minutes and then replaced the gun in its wrapper and sat down at the card table to go over her plans.

Nora Jane had a methodical streak and liked to take care of details.

II

'The first nigger that comes in here attempting a robbery is going to be in the wrong place,' Jody laughed, smiling at Judge Crozier and handing him a fresh bourbon and Coke across the bar.

'Yes, sir, that nigger is gonna be in the wrong place.' Jody fingered the blackjack that lay in its purple velvet sack on a small shelf below the antiquated cash register and warmed into his favourite subject, his interest in local crime fuelled by a report in the *Times–Picayune* of a holdup in a neighbourhood Tote-Sum store.

The black bandits had made the customers lie on the floor, cleaned out the cash register, and helped themselves to a cherry Icee on the way out. The newspaper carried a photograph of the Icee machine.

The judge popped open his third sack of Bar-B-Que potato chips and looked thoughtful. The other customers waited politely to see what he had to say for himself this morning concerning law and order.

'Now, Jody, you don't know how a man will act in an emergency until that emergency transpires,' the judge began, wiping his hands on his worn seersucker pants. 'That's a fact and worthy of all good men to be accepted. Your wife could be in here helping tend bar. Your tables could be full of innocent customers watching a ball game. You might be busy talking to someone like that sweet little girl who came in last Saturday collecting for the Crippled Children's Hospital. First thing you know, gun in your back, knife at your throat. It has nothing at all to do with being brave.' The judge polished off his drink and turned to look out the door to where the poll was going on.

Jody's Bar didn't cater to just anyone that happened to drop by to get a drink or lay a bet. It was the oldest neighbourhood bar in the Irish Channel section of New Orleans, and its regular customers included second- and third-generation drinkers from many walks of life. Descendants of Creole blue bloods mingled easily with house painters and deliverymen stopping by for a quick one on their route.

Jody ran a notoriously tight ship. No one but Jody himself had ever answered the telephone that sat beneath a framed copy of The Auburn Creed, and no woman, no matter what her tale of woe, had ever managed to get him to call a man to the phone.

'Not here,' he would answer curtly, 'haven't seen him.' And Jody would hang up without offering to take a message. If a woman wanted a man at Jody's, she had to come look for him in person.

There was an air of anticipation around Jody's this Saturday morning. All eight of the stools were filled. The excitement was due to the poll.

Outside of Jody's, seated at a small card table underneath a green-and-white-striped awning, Wesley Labouisse was proceeding with the poll in a businesslike manner. Every male passerby was interviewed in turn and his ballot folded into quarters and deposited in the Mason jar with a pink ribbon from an old Valentine's box wrapped loosely around it.

'Just mark it yes or no. Whatever advice you would give your closest friend if he came to you and told you he was thinking of getting married.' Wesley was talking to a fourteen-year-old boy straddling a ten-speed bike.

'Take all the time you need to make up your mind. Think about your mother and father. Think about what it's like to have a woman tell you when to come home every night and when to get up in the morning and when to take a bath and when to talk and when to shut up. Think about what it's like to give your money to a woman from now till the day you die. Then just write down your honest feelings about whether a perfectly happy man ought to go out and get himself married.'

Wesley was in a good mood. He had thought up the poll himself and had side bets laid all the way from The New

Orleans Country Club to the Plaquemines Parish sheriff's office.

There was a big sign tacked up over the card table declaring THIS POLL IS BEING CONDUCTED WITHOUT REGARD TO SEX OR PREVIOUS CONDITION OF SERVITUDE. Wesley had made the sign himself and thought it was hilarious. He was well known in New Orleans society as the author of Boston Club Mardi Gras skits.

The leading man in the drama of the poll, Prescott Hamilton IV, was leaning into Jody's pinball machine with the dedication of a ballet dancer winding up *The Firebird*. He was twelve games ahead and his brand-new, navy blue wedding suit hung in its plastic see-through wrapper on the edge of the machine swaying in rhythm as Prescott nudged the laws of pinball machines gently in his favour. He was a lucky gambler and an ace pinball-machine player. He was a general favourite at Jody's, where the less aristocratic customers loved him for his gentle ways and his notoriously hollow leg.

Prescott wasn't pretending to be more interested in the outcome of the pinball-machine game than in the outcome of the poll that was deciding his matrimonial future. He was genuinely more interested in the pinball machine. Prescott had great powers of concentration and was a man who lived in the present.

Prescott didn't really care whether he married Emily Ann Hughes or not. He and Emily Ann had been getting along fine for years without getting married, and he didn't see what difference his moving into Emily Ann's house at this late date was going to make in the history of the world.

Besides he wasn't certain how his Labradors would adjust to her backyard. Emily Anne's house was nice, but the yard was full of little fences and lacked a shade tree.

Nonetheless, Prescott was a man of his word, and if the poll came out in favour of marriage they would be married as soon as he could change into his suit and find an Episcopal minister, unless Emily Ann would be reasonable and settle for the judge.

Prescott was forty-eight years old. The wild blood of his pioneer ancestors had slowed down in Prescott. Even his smile took a long time to develop, feeling out the terrain, then opening up like a child's.

'Crime wave, crime wave, that's all I hear around this place anymore,' the judge muttered, tapping his cigar on the edge of the bar and staring straight at the rack of potato chips. 'Let's talk about something else for a change.'

'Judge, you ought to get Jody to take you back to the ladies' room and show you the job Claiborne did of patching the window so kids on the street can't see into the ladies',' one of the regulars said. Two or three guys laughed, holding their stomachs.

'Claiborne owed Jody sixty bucks on his tab and the window was broken out in the ladies' room so Jody's old lady talked him into letting Claiborne fix the window to pay back part of the money he owes. After all, Claiborne is supposed to be a carpenter.' Everyone started laughing again.

'Well, Claiborne showed up about six sheets in the wind last Wednesday while Jody was out jogging in the park and he went to work. You wouldn't believe what he did. He boarded up the window. He didn't feel like going out for a window-pane, so he just boarded up the window with scrap lumber.'

'I'll have to see that as soon as it calms down around here,' the judge said, and he turned to watch Prescott who was staring passionately into the lighted TILT sign on the pinball machine.

'What's wrong, Prescott,' he said, 'you losing your touch?'

'Could be, Judge,' Prescott answered, slipping another quarter into the slot.

The late afternoon sun shone in the windows of the bare apartment. Nora Jane had dumped most of her possessions into a container for The Volunteers of America. She had even burned Sandy's letters. If she was caught there was no sense in involving him.

If she was caught what could they do to her, a young girl, a first offender, the daughter of a hero? The sisters would come to her rescue. Nora Jane had carefully been attending early morning mass for several weeks.

She trembled with excitement and glanced at her watch. She shook her head and walked over to the mirror on the dresser. Nora Jane couldn't decide if she was frightened or not. She looked deep into her eyes in the mirror trying to read the secrets of her mind, but Nora Jane was too much in love to even know her own secrets. She was inside a mystery deeper than the mass.

She inspected the reddish-blonde wig with its cascades of silky Dynel falling around her shoulders and blinked her black eyelashes. To the wig and eyelashes she added blue eye shadow, peach rouge and beige lipstick. Nora Jane looked awful.

'You look like a piece of shit,' she said to her reflection, adding another layer of lipstick. 'Anyway, it's time to go.'

On weekends six o'clock was the slow hour at Jody's, when most of the customers went home to change for the evening.

Nora Jane walked down the two flights of stairs and out onto the sidewalk carrying the brown leather bag. Inside was her costume change and a bus ticket to San Francisco zippered into the side compartment. The gun was stuffed into one of the Red Cross shoes she had bought to wear with the short brown nun's habit she had stolen from Dominican College. She hoped the short veil wasn't getting wrinkled. Nora Jane was prissy about her appearance.

As she walked along in the August evening she dreamed of Sandy sitting on her bed playing his harmonica while she pretended to sleep. In the dream he was playing an old Bob Dylan love song, the sort of thing she liked to listen to before he upgraded her taste in music.

Earlier that afternoon Nora Jane had rolled a pair of shorts, an old shirt, and some sandals into a neat bundle and hidden it in the low-hanging branches of the oak tree where Sandy had planted her money.

A scrawny-looking black kid was dozing in the roots of the tree. He promised to keep an eye on her things.

'If I don't come back by tomorrow afternoon you can have this stuff,' she told him. 'The sandals were handmade in Brazil.'

'Thanks,' the black kid said. 'I'll watch it for you till then. You running away from home or what?'

'I'm going to rob a bank,' she confided.

The black kid giggled and shot her the old peace sign.

Wesley walked into the bar where Prescott, Jody, and the judge were all alone watching the evening news on television.

'Aren't you getting tired of that goddamn poll,' Prescott said to him. 'Emily Anne won't even answer her phone. A joke's a joke, Wesley. I better put on my suit and get on over there.'

'Not yet,' Wesley said. 'The sun isn't all the way down yet. Wait till we open the jar. You promised.' Prescott was drunk, but Wesley was drunker. Not that either of them ever showed their whisky.

'I promised I wouldn't get married unless you found one boy or man all day who thought it was an unqualified good idea to get married. I didn't ever say I was interested in waiting around for the outcome of a vote. Come on and open up that jar before Emily Anne gets any madder.'

'What makes you think there is a single ballot in favour of you getting married?' Wesley asked.

'I don't know if there is or there isn't,' Prescott answered. 'So go on and let the judge open that goddamn jar.'

'Look at him, Wesley,' Jody said, delightedly. 'He ain't even signed the papers yet and he's already acting like a married man. Already worried about getting home in time for dinner. If Miss Emily Anne Hughes wakes up in the morning wearing a ring from Prescott, I say she takes the cake. I say she's gone and caught a whale on a ten-pound test line.'

'Open the jar,' Prescott demanded, while the others howled with laughter.

Nora Jane stepped into the bar, closed the door behind her, and turned the lock. She kept the pistol pointed at the four men who were clustered around the cash register.

'Please be quiet and put your hands over your heads before I kill one of you,' she said politely, waving the gun with one hand and reaching behind herself with the other to draw the window shade that said CLOSED in red letters.

Prescott and the judge raised their hands first, then Wesley.

'Do as you are told,' the judge said to Jody in his deep voice. 'Jody, do what that woman tells you to do and do it this instant.' Jody added his hands to the six already pointing at the ceiling fan.

'Get in there,' Nora Jane directed, indicating the ladies' room at the end of the bar. 'Please hurry before you make me angry. I ran away from DePaul's Hospital yesterday afternoon and I haven't had my medication and I become angry very easily.'

The judge held the door open, and the four men crowded into the small bathroom.

'Face the window,' Nora Jane ordered, indicating Claiborne's famous repair job. The astonished men obeyed silently as she closed the bathroom door and turned the skeleton key in its lock and dropped it on the floor under the bar.

'Please be very quiet so I won't get worried and need to shoot through the door,' she said. 'Be awfully quiet. I am an alcoholic and I need some of this whisky. I need some whisky in the worst way.'

Nora Jane changed into the nun's habit, wiping the makeup off her face with a bar rag and stuffing the old clothes into the bag. Next she opened the cash register, removed all the bills without counting them, and dropped them into the bag. On second thought she added the pile of IOUs and walked back to the door of the ladies' room.

'Please be a little quieter,' she said in a husky voice. 'I'm getting very nervous.'

'Don't worry, Miss. We are cooperating to the fullest extent,' the judge's bench voice answered.

'That's nice,' Nora Jane said. 'That's very nice.'

She pinned the little veil to her hair, picked up the bag, and walked out the door. She looked all around, but there was no one on the street but a couple of kids riding tricycles.

As she passed the card table she stopped, marked a ballot, folded it neatly, and dropped it into the Mason jar.

Then, like a woman in a dream, she walked on down the street, the rays of the setting sun making her a path all the way to the bus stop at the corner of Annunciation and Nashville Avenue.

Making her path all the way to mountains and valleys and fields, to rivers and streams and oceans. To a boy who was like no other. To the source of all water.

IN THE LAND OF DREAMY DREAMS

On 3 May 1977, LaGrande McGruder drove out on to the Huey P. Long Bridge, dropped two Davis Classics and a gut-strung PDP tournament racket into the Mississippi River, and quit playing tennis for ever.

'That was it,' she said. 'That was the last goddamn straw.' She heaved a sigh, thinking this must be what it feels like to die, to be through with something that was more trouble than it was worth.

As long as she could remember LaGrande had been playing tennis four or five hours a day whenever it wasn't raining or she didn't have a funeral to attend. In her father's law office was a whole cabinet full of her trophies.

After the rackets sank La Grande dumped a can of brand-new Slazenger tennis balls into the river and stood for a long time watching the cheerful, little, yellow constellation form and re-form in the muddy current.

'Jesus Fucking A Christ,' she said to herself. 'Oh, well,' she added, 'maybe now I can get my arms to be the same size for the first time in my life.'

La Grande leaned into the bridge railing, staring past the white circles on her wrists, souvenirs of twenty years of wearing sweatbands in the fierce New Orleans sunlight, and on down to the river where the little yellow constellation was overtaking a barge.

'That goddamn little new-rich Yankee bitch,' she said, kicking the bridge with her leather Tretorns.

There was no denying it. There was no undoing it. At ten o'clock that morning LaGrande McGruder, whose grandfather had been president of the United States Lawn Tennis Association, had cheated a crippled girl out of a tennis match, had deliberately and without hesitation made a bad call in the last point of a crucial game, had defended the call against loud protests, taken a big drink of her Gatorade, and proceeded to win the next twelve games while her opponent reeled with disbelief at being done out of her victory.

At exactly three minutes after ten that morning she had looked across the net at the impassive face of the interloper who was about to humiliate her at her own tennis club and she had changed her mind about honour quicker than the speed of light. 'Out,' she had said, not giving a damn whether the serve was in or out. 'Nice try.'

'It couldn't be out,' the crippled girl said. 'Are you sure?'

'Of course I'm sure,' La Grande said. 'I wouldn't have called it unless I was sure.'

'Are you positive?' the crippled girl said.

'For God's sake,' La Grande said, 'look, if you don't mind, let's hurry up and get this over with. I have to be at the country club for lunch.' That ought to get her, LaGrande thought. At least they don't let Jews into the country club yet. At least that's still sacred.

'Serving,' the crippled girl said, trying to control her rage.

LaGrande took her position at the back of the court, reaching up to adjust her visor, and caught the eye of old Claiborne Redding, who was sitting on the second-floor balcony watching the match. He smiled and waved. How long has he been standing there, La Grande wondered. How long has that old fart been watching me? But she was too busy to worry about Claiborne now. She had a tennis match to save, and she was going to save it if it was the last thing she ever did in her life.

The crippled girl set her mouth into a tight line and prepared to serve into the forehand court. Her name was Roxanne Miller, and she had travelled a long way to this morning's fury. She had spent thousands of dollars on private tennis lessons, hundreds of dollars on equipment, and untold time and energy giving cocktail parties and dinner parties for the entrenched players who one by one she had courted and blackmailed and finagled into giving her matches and return matches until finally one day she would catch them at a weak moment and defeat them. She kept a mental list of such victories. Sometimes when she went to bed at night she would pull the pillows over her head and lie there imagining herself as a sort of Greek figure of justice, sitting on a marble chair in the clouds, holding a scroll, a little parable of conquest and revenge.

It had taken Roxanne five years to fight and claw and worm her way into the ranks of respected Lawn Tennis Club Ladies. For five years she had dragged her bad foot around the carefully manicured courts of the oldest and snottiest tennis club in the United States of America.

For months now her ambitions had centred around LaGrande. A victory over LaGrande would mean she had arrived in the top echelons of the Lawn Tennis Club Ladies.

A victory over LaGrande would surely be followed by invitations to play in the top doubles games, perhaps even in the famous Thursday foursome that played on Rena Clark's private tennis court. Who knows, Roxanne dreamed, LaGrande might even ask her to be her doubles partner. LaGrande's old doubles partners were always retiring to have babies. At any moment she might need a new one. Roxanne would be there waiting, the indefatigable handicapped wonder of the New Orleans tennis world.

She had envisioned this morning's victory a thousand times, had seen herself walking up to the net to shake LaGrande's hand, had planned her little speech of condolence, after which the two of them would go into the snack bar for lunch and have a heart-to-heart talk about rackets and balls and backhands and forehands and volleys and lobs.

Roxanne basked in her dreams. It did not bother her that LaGrande never returned her phone calls, avoided her at the club, made vacant replies to her requests for matches. Roxanne had plenty of time. She could wait. Sooner or later she could catch LaGrande in a weak moment.

That moment came at the club's 100th Anniversary Celebration. Everyone was drunk and full of camaraderie. The old members were all on their best behaviour, trying to be extra nice to the new members and pretend like the new members were just as good as they were even if they didn't belong to the Boston Club or the Southern Yacht Club or Comus or Momus or Proteus.

Roxanne cornered LaGrande while she was talking to a famous psychiatrist-player from Washington, a bachelor who was much adored in tennis circles for his wit and political connections.

La Grande was trying to impress him with how sane she was and hated to let him see her irritation when Roxanne moved in on them.

'When are you going to give me that match you promised me?' Roxanne asked, looking wistful, as if this were something the two of them had been discussing for years.

'I don't know,' LaGrande said. 'I guess I just stay so busy. This is Semmes Talbot, from Washington. This is Roxanne,

Semmes. I'm sorry. I can't remember your last name. You'll have to help me.'

'Miller,' Roxanne said. 'My name is Miller. Really now, when will you play with me?'

'Well, how about Monday?' LaGrande heard herself saying. 'I guess I could do it Monday. My doubles game was cancelled.' She looked up at the doctor to see if he appreciated how charming she was to everyone, no matter who they were.

'Fine,' Roxanne said. 'Monday's fine. I'll be here at nine. I'll be counting on it so don't let me down.' She laughed. 'I thought you'd never say yes. I was beginning to think you were afraid I'd beat you.'

'Oh, my goodness,' LaGrande said, 'anyone can beat me, I don't take tennis very seriously any more, you know. I just play enough to keep my hand in.'

'Who was that?' Semmes asked when Roxanne left them. 'She certainly has her nerve!'

'She's one of the new members,' LaGrande said. 'I really try so hard not to be snotty about them. I really do believe that every human being is just as valuable as everyone else, don't you? And it doesn't matter a bit to me what anyone's background is, but some of the new people are sort of hard to take. They're so, oh, well, so *eager*.'

Semmes looked down the front of her silk blouse and laughed happily into her aristocratic eyes. 'Well, watch out for that one,' he said. 'There's no reason for anyone as pretty as you to let people make you uncomfortable.'

Across the room Roxanne collected Willie and got ready to leave the party. She was on her way home to begin training for the match.

Willie was glad to leave. He didn't like hanging around places where he wasn't wanted. He couldn't imagine why

Roxanne wanted to spent all her time playing tennis with a bunch of snotty people.

Roxanne and Willie were new members. Willie's brand-new 15 million dollars and the New Orleans Lawn Tennis Club's brand-new $700,000 dollar mortgage had met at a point in history, and Willie's application for membership had been approved by the board and railroaded past the watchful noses of old Claiborne Redding and his buddies. Until then the only Jewish member of the club had been a globe-trotting Jewish bachelor who knew his wines, entertained lavishly at Antoine's, and had the courtesy to stay in Europe most of the time.

Willie and Roxanne were something else again. 'What in the hell are we going to do with a guy who sells ties and a crippled woman who runs around Audubon Park all day in a pair of tennis shorts,' Claiborne said, pulling on a pair of the thick white Australian wool socks he wore to play in. The committee had cornered him in the locker room.

'The membership's not for him,' they said. 'He doesn't even play. You'll never see him. And she really isn't a cripple. One leg is a little bit shorter than the other one, that's all.'

'I don't know,' Claiborne said. 'Not just Jews, for God's sake, but Yankee Jews to boot.'

'The company's listed on the American Stock Exchange, Claiborne. It was selling at sixteen-and-a-half this morning, up from five. And he buys his insurance from me. Come on, you'll never see them. All she's going to do is play a little tennis with the ladies.'

Old Claiborne rued the day he had let himself be talked into Roxanne and Willie. The club had been forced to take in thirty new families to pay for its new building and some of them were Jews, but, as Claiborne was fond of saying, at least the rest of them tried to act like white people.

46

Roxanne was something else. It seemed to him that she lived at the club. The only person who hung around the club more than Roxanne was old Claiborne himself. Pretty soon she was running the place. She wrote *The Lawn Tennis Newsletter*. She circulated petitions to change the all-white dress rule. She campaigned for more court privileges for women. She dashed in and out of the bar and the dining room making plans with the waiters and chefs for Mixed Doubles Nights, Round Robin Galas, Benefit Children's Jamborees, Saturday Night Luaus.

Claiborne felt like his club was being turned into a cruise ship.

On top of everything else Roxanne was always trying to get in good with Claiborne. Every time he settled down on the balcony to watch a match she came around trying to talk to him, talking while the match was going on, remembering the names of his grandchildren, complimenting him on their serves and backhands and footwork, taking every conceivable liberty, as if at any moment she might start showing up at their weddings and débuts.

Claiborne thought about Roxanne a lot. He was thinking about her this morning when he arrived at the club and saw her cream-coloured Rolls Royce blocking his view of the Garth Humphries Memorial Plaque. He was thinking about her as he got a cup of coffee from a stand the ladies had taken to setting up by the sign-in board. This was some more of her meddling, he thought, percolated coffee in Styrofoam cups with plastic spoons and some kind of powder instead of cream.

At the old clubhouse waiters had brought steaming cups of thick chicory-flavoured café au lait out onto the balcony with cream and sugar in silver servers.

Claiborne heaved a sigh, pulled his pants out of his crotch, and went up to the balcony to see what the morning would bring.

He had hardly reached the top of the stairs when he saw Roxanne leading LaGrande to a deserted court at the end of the property. My God in Heaven, he thought, how did she pull that off? How in the name of God did she get hold of Leland's daughter?

Leland McGruder had been Claiborne's doubles partner in their youth. Together they had known victory and defeat in New Orleans and Jackson and Monroe and Shreveport and Mobile and Atlanta and as far away as Forest Hills during one never-to-be-forgotten year when they had thrown their rackets into a red Ford and gone off together on the tour.

Down on the court LaGrande was so aggravated she could barely be civil. How did I end up here, she thought, playing second-class tennis against anyone who corners me at a party.

LaGrande was in a bad mood all around. The psychiatrist had squired her around all weekend, fucked her dispassionately in someone's *garçonnière*, and gone back to Washington without making further plans to see her.

She bounced a ball up and down a few times with her racket, thinking about a line of poetry that kept occurring to her lately whenever she played tennis. 'Their only monument the asphalt road, and a thousand lost goft balls.'

'Are you coming to Ladies Day on Wednesday?' Roxanne was saying, 'We're going to have a great time. You really ought to come. We've got a real clown coming to give out helium balloons, and we're going to photograph the winners sitting on his lap for the newsletter. Isn't that a cute idea?'

'I'm afraid I'm busy Wednesday,' LaGrande said, imagining balloons flying all over the courts when the serious players arrived for their noon games. 'Look,' she said, 'let's go on and get started. I can't stay too long.'

They set down their pitchers of Gatorade, put on their visors and sweatbands, sprayed a little powdered resin on their hands, and walked out to their respective sides of the court.

Before they hit the ball four times LaGrande knew something was wrong. The woman wasn't going to warm her up! LaGrande had hit her three nice long smooth balls and each time Roxanne moved up to the net and put the ball away on the sidelines.

'How about hitting me some forehands,' LaGrande said. 'I haven't played in a week. I need to warm up.'

'I'll try,' Roxanne said, 'I have to play most of my game at the net, you know, because of my leg.'

'Well, stay back there and hit me some to warm up with,' LaGrande said, but Roxanne went right on putting her shots away with an assortment of tricks that looked more like a circus act than a tennis game.

'Are you ready to play yet?' she asked. 'I'd like to get started before I get too tired.'

'Sure,' LaGrande said. 'Go ahead, you serve first. There's no reason to spin a racket over a fun match.' Oh, well, she thought, I'll just go ahead and slaughter her. Of course, I won't lob over her head, I don't suppose anyone does that to her.

Roxanne pulled the first ball out of her pants. She had a disconcerting habit of sticking the extra ball up the leg of her tights instead of keeping it in a pocket. She pulled the ball out of her pants, tossed it expertly up into the air, and served an ace to LaGrande's extreme backhand service corner.

'Nice serve,' LaGrande said. Oh, well, she thought, everyone gets one off occasionally. Let her go on and get overconfident. Then I can get this over in a hurry.

They changed courts for the second serve. Roxanne hit

short into the backhand court. LaGrande raced up and hit a forehand right into Roxanne's waiting racket. The ball dropped neatly into a corner and the score was 30–love.

How in the shit did she get to the net so fast, LaGrande thought. Well, I'll have to watch out for that. I thought she was supposed to be crippled.

Roxanne served again, winning the point with a short spinning forehand. Before LaGrande could gather her wits about her she had lost the first game.

Things went badly with her serve and she lost the second game. While she was still recovering from that she lost the third game. Calm down, she told herself. Get hold of yourself. Keep your eye on the ball. Anticipate her moves. It's only because I didn't have a chance to warm up. I'll get going in a minute.

Old Claiborne stood watching the match from a secluded spot near the door to the dining room, watching it with his heart in his throat, not daring to move any farther out onto the balcony for fear he might distract LaGrande and make things worse.

Why doesn't she lob, Claiborne thought. Why in the name of God doesn't she lob? Maybe she thinks she shouldn't do it just because one of that woman's legs is a little bit shorter than the other.

He stood up squeezing the Styrofoam cup in his hand. A small hole had developed in the side, and drops of coffee were making a little track down the side of his Fred Perry flannels, but he was oblivious to everything but the action on the court.

He didn't even notice when Nailor came up behind him. Nailor was a haughty old black man who had been with the club since he was a young boy and now was the chief groundskeeper and arbiter of manners among the hired help.

Nailor had spent his life tending Rubico tennis courts

without once having the desire to pick up a racket. But he had watched thousands of tennis matches and he knew more about tennis than most players did.

He knew how the little fields of energy that surround men and women move and coalesce and strike and fend off and retreat and attack and conquer. That was what he looked for when he watched tennis. He wasn't interested in the details.

If it was up to Nailor no one but a few select players would ever be allowed to set foot on his Rubico courts. The only time of day when he was really at peace was the half hour from when he finished the courts around 7.15 each morning until they opened the iron gates at 7.45 and the members started arriving.

Nailor had known LaGrande since she came to her father's matches in a perambulator. He had lusted after her ass ever since she got her first white tennis skirt and her first Wilson autograph racket. He had been the first black man to wax her first baby-blue convertible, and he had been taking care of her cars ever since.

Nailor moonlighted at the club polishing cars with a special wax he had invented.

Nailor hated the new members worse than Claiborne did. Ever since the club had moved to its new quarters and they had come crowding in bringing their children and leaving their paper cups all over the courts he had been thinking of retiring.

Now he was watching one of them taking his favourite little missy to the cleaners. She's getting her little booty whipped for sure this morning, he thought. She can't find a place to turn and make a stand. She don't know where to start to stop it. She's got hind teat today whether she likes it or not and I'm glad her daddy's not here to watch it.

Claiborne was oblivious to Nailor. He was trying to decide

who would benefit most if he made a show of walking out to the balcony and taking a seat.

He took a chance. He waited until LaGrande's back was to him, then walked out just as Roxanne was receiving serve.

LaGrande made a small rally and won her service, but Roxanne took the next three games for the set. 'I don't need to rest between sets unless you do,' she said, walking up to the net. 'We really haven't been playing that long. I really don't know why I'm playing so well. I guess I'm just lucky today.'

'I guess you are,' LaGrande said. 'Sure, let's go right on. I've got a date for lunch.' Now I'll take her, she thought. Now I'm tired of being polite. Now I'm going to beat the shit out of her.

Roxanne picked up a ball, tossed it into the air, and served another ace into the backhand corner of the forehand court.

Jesus Fucking A Christ, LaGrande thought. She did it again. Where in the name of God did that little Jewish housewife learn that shot.

LaGrande returned the next serve with a lob. Roxanne ran back, caught it on the edge of her racket and dribbled it over the net.

Now LaGrande lost all powers of reason. She began trying to kill the ball on every shot. Before she could get hold of herself she had lost three games, then four, then five, then she was only one game away from losing the match, then only one point.

This is it, LaGrande thought. Armageddon.

Roxanne picked up the balls and served the first one out. She slowed herself down, took a deep breath, tossed up the second ball and shot a clean forehand into the service box.

'Out,' LaGrande said. 'Nice try.'

'It couldn't be out,' Roxanne said. 'Are you sure?'

'Of course I'm sure,' LaGrande said. '*I wouldn't have called it unless I was sure.*'

Up on the balcony old Claiborne's heart was opening and closing like a geisha's fan. He caught LaGrande's eye, smiled and waved, and, turning around, realized that Nailor was standing behind him.

'Morning, Mr Claiborne,' Nailor said, leaning politely across him to pick up the cup. 'Looks like Mr Leland's baby's having herself a hard time this morning. Let me bring you something nice to drink while you watch.'

Claiborne sent him for coffee and settled back in the chair to watch LaGrande finish her off, thinking, as he often did lately, that he had outlived his time and his place. 'I'm not suited for a holding action,' he told himself, imagining the entire culture of the white Christian world to be stretched out on some sort of endless Maginot line besieged by the children of the poor carrying portable radios and boxes of fried chicken.

Here Claiborne sat, on a beautiful spring morning, in good spirits, still breathing normally, his blood coursing through his veins on its admirable and accustomed journeys, and only a few minutes before he had been party to a violation of a code he had lived by all his life.

He sat there, sipping his tasteless coffee, listening to the Saturday lawn mowers starting up on the lawn of the Poydras Retirement Home, which took up the other half of the square block of prime New Orleans real estate on which the new clubhouse was built. It was a very exclusive old folks' home, with real antiques and Persian rugs and a board of directors made up of members of the New Orleans Junior League. Some of the nicest old people in New Orleans went there to die.

Claiborne had suffered through a series of terrible luncheons at the Poydras Home in an effort to get them to allow the tennis club to unlock one of the gates that separated the two properties. But no matter how the board of directors of the Lawn Tennis Club pleaded and bargained and implored, the board of directors of the Poydras Home stoutly refused to allow the tennis-club members to set foot on their lawn to retrieve the balls that flew over the fence. A ball lost to the Poydras Home was a ball gone forever.

The old-fashioned steel girders of the Huey P. Long Bridge hung languidly in the moist air. The sun beat down on the river. The low-hanging clouds pushed against each other in fat cosmic orgasms.

LaGrande stood on the bridge until the constellation of yellow balls was out of sight around a bend in the river. Then she drove to her house on Philip Street, changed clothes, got in the car, and began to drive aimlessly up and down Saint Charles Avenue, thinking of things to do with the rest of her life.

She decided to cheer herself up. She turned onto Carrollton Avenue and drove down to Gus Mayer.

She went in, found a sales lady, took up a large dressing room, and bought some cocktail dresses and some sun dresses and some summer skirts and blouses and some pink linen pants and a beige silk Calvin Klein evening jacket.

Then she went downstairs and bought some hose and some makeup and some perfume and some brassières and some panties and a blue satin Christian Dior gown and robe.

She went into the shoe department and bought some Capezio sandals and some Bass loafers and some handmade espadrilles. She bought a red umbrella and a navy blue canvas handbag.

When she had bought one each of every single thing she could possibly imagine needing she felt better and went on out to the Country Club to see if anyone she liked to fuck was hanging around the pool.

REVENGE

It was the summer of the Broad Jump Pit.

The Broad Jump Pit, how shall I describe it! It was a bright orange rectangle in the middle of a green pasture. It was three feet deep, filled with river sand and sawdust. A real cinder track led up to it, ending where tall poles for pole-vaulting rose for ever in the still Delta air.

I am looking through the old binoculars. I am watching Bunky coming at a run down the cinder path, pausing expertly at the jump-off line, then rising into the air, heels stretched far out in front of him, landing in the sawdust. Before the dust has settled St John comes running with the tape, calling out measurements in his high, excitable voice.

Next comes my thirteen-year-old brother, Dudley, coming at a brisk jog down the track, the pole-vaulting pole held lightly in his delicate hands, then vaulting, high into the sky. His skinny tanned legs make a last, desperate surge, and he is clear and over.

Think how it looked from my lonely exile atop the chicken house. I was ten years old, the only girl in a house full of cousins. There were six of us, shipped to the Delta for the summer, dumped on my grandmother right in the middle of a world war.

They built this wonder in answer to a V-Mail letter from my father in Europe. The war was going well, my father wrote, within a year the Allies would triumph over the forces of evil, the world would be at peace, and the Olympic torch would again be brought down from its mountain and carried to Zurich or Amsterdam or London or Mexico City, wherever free men lived and worshipped sports. My father had been a participant in an Olympic event when he was young.

Therefore, the letter continued, Dudley and Bunky and Philip and St John and Oliver were to begin training. The United States would need athletes now, not soldiers.

They were to train for broad jumping and pole-vaulting and discus throwing, for fifty-, one-hundred-, and four-hundred-yard dashes, for high and low hurdles. The letter included instructions for building the pit, for making pole-vaulting poles out of cane, and for converting ordinary sawhorses into hurdles. It ended with a page of tips for proper eating and admonished Dudley to take good care of me as I was my father's own dear sweet little girl.

The letter came one afternoon. Early the next morning they began construction. Around noon I wandered out to the pasture to see how they were coming along. I picked up a shovel.

'Put that down, Rhoda,' Dudley said. 'Don't bother us now. We're working.'

'I know it,' I said. 'I'm going to help.'

'No, you're not,' Bunky said. 'This is the Broad Jump Pit. We're starting our training.'

'I'm going to do it too,' I said. 'I'm going to be in training.'

'Get out of here now,' Dudley said. 'This is only for boys, Rhoda. This isn't a game.'

'I'm going to dig it if I want to,' I said, picking up a shovelful of dirt and throwing it on Philip. On second thought I picked up another shovelful and threw it on Bunky.

'Get out of here, Ratface,' Philip yelled at me. 'You German spy.' He was referring to the initials on my Girl Scout uniform.

'You goddamn niggers,' I yelled. 'You niggers. I'm digging this if I want to and you can't stop me, you nasty niggers, you Japs, you Jews.' I was throwing dirt on everyone now. Dudley grabbed the shovel and wrestled me to the ground. He held my arms down in the coarse grass and peered into my face.

'Rhoda, you're not having anything to do with this Broad Jump Pit. And if you set foot inside this pasture or come around here and touch anything we will break your legs and drown you in the bayou with a crowbar around your neck.' He was twisting my leg until it creaked at the joints. 'Do you get it, Rhoda? Do you understand me?'

'Let me up,' I was screaming, my rage threatening to split open my skull. 'Let me up, you goddamn nigger, you Jap, you spy. I'm telling Grannie and you're going to get the worst whipping of your life. And you better quit digging this hole for the horses to fall in. Let me up, let me up. Let me go.'

'You've been ruining everything we've thought up all summer,' Dudley said, 'and you're not setting foot inside this pasture.'

In the end they dragged me back to the house, and I ran screaming into the kitchen where Grannie and Calvin, the black man who did the cooking, tried to comfort me, feeding me pound cake and offering to let me help with the mayonnaise.

'You be a sweet girl, Rhoda,' my grandmother said, 'and this afternoon we'll go over to Eisenglas Plantation to play with Miss Ann Wentzel.'

'I don't want to play with Miss Ann Wentzel,' I screamed. 'I hate Miss Ann Wentzel. She's fat and she calls me a Yankee. She said my socks were ugly.'

'Why, Rhoda,' my grandmother said. 'I'm surprised at you.

57

Miss Ann Wentzel is your own sweet friend. Her momma was
your momma's roommate at All Saint's. How can you talk like
that?'

'She's a nigger,' I screamed. 'She's a goddamned nigger
German spy.'

'Now it's coming. Here comes the temper,' Calvin said,
rolling his eyes back in their sockets to make me madder. I
threw my second fit of the morning, beating my fists into a
door frame. My grandmother seized me in soft arms. She led
me to a bedroom where I sobbed myself to sleep in a sea of
down pillows.

The construction went on for several weeks. As soon as they
finished breakfast every morning they started out for the
pasture. Wood had to be burned to make cinders, sawdust
brought from the sawmill, sand hauled up from the riverbank
by wheelbarrow.

When the pit was finished the savage training began. From
my several vantage points I watched them. Up and down, up
and down they ran, dove, flew, sprinted. Drenched with
sweat they wrestled each other to the ground in bitter feuds
over distances and times and fractions of inches.

Dudley was their self-appointed leader. He drove them like
a demon. They began each morning by running around the
edge of the pasture several times, then practising their hurdles
and dashes, then on to discus throwing and calisthenics. Then
on to the Broad Jump Pit with its endless challenges.

They even pressed the old mare into service. St John was
from New Orleans and knew the British Ambassador and was
thinking of being a polo player. Up and down the pasture he
drove the poor old creature, leaning far out of the saddle,
swatting a basketball with my grandaddy's cane.

I spied on them from the swing that went out over the bayou, and from the roof of the chicken house, and sometimes from the pasture fence itself, calling out insults or attempts to make them jealous.

'Guess what,' I would yell, 'I'm going to town to the Chinaman's store.' 'Guess what, I'm getting to go to the beauty parlour.' 'Doctor Biggs says you're adopted.'

They ignored me. At meals they sat together at one end of the table, making jokes about my temper and my red hair, opening their mouths so I could see their half-chewed food, burping loudly in my direction.

At night they pulled their cots together on the sleeping porch, plotting against me while I slept beneath my grand-mother's window, listening to the soft assurance of her snoring.

I began to pray the Japs would win the war, would come marching into Issaquena County and take them prisoners, starving and torturing them, sticking bamboo splinters under their fingernails. I saw myself in the Japanese colonel's office, turning them in, writing their names down, myself being treated like an honoured guest, drinking tea from tiny blue cups like the ones the Chinaman had in his store.

They would be outside, tied up with wire. There would be Dudley, begging for mercy. What good to him now his loyal gang, his photographic memory, his trick magnet dogs, his perfect pitch, his camp shorts, his Baby Brownie camera.

I prayed they would get polio, would be consigned forever to iron lungs. I put myself to sleep at night imagining their laboured breathing, their five little wheelchairs lined up by the store as I drove by in my father's Packard, my arm around the jacket of his blue uniform, on my way to Hollywood for my screen test.

*

Meanwhile, I practised dancing. My grandmother had a black housekeeper named Baby Doll who was a wonderful dancer. In the mornings I followed her around while she dusted, begging for dancing lessons. She was a big woman, as tall as a man, and gave off a dark rich smell, an unforgettable incense, a combination of Evening in Paris and the sweet perfume of the cabins.

Baby Doll wore bright skirts and on her blouses a pin that said REMEMBER, then a real pearl, then HARBOR. She was engaged to a sailor and was going to California to be rich as soon as the war was over.

I would put a stack of heavy, scratched records on the record player, and Baby Doll and I would dance through the parlours to the music of Glenn Miller or Guy Lombardo or Tommy Dorsey.

Sometimes I stood on a stool in front of the fireplace and made up lyrics while Baby Doll acted them out, moving lightly across the old dark rugs, turning and swooping and shaking and gliding.

Outside the summer sun beat down on the Delta, beating down a million volts a minute, feeding the soybeans and cotton and clover, sucking Steele's Bayou up into the clouds, beating down on the road and the store, on the pecans and elms and magnolias, on the men at work in the fields, on the athletes at work in the pasture.

Inside Baby Doll and I would be dancing. Or Guy Lombardo would be playing 'Begin the Beguine' and I would be belting out lyrics.

Oh, let them begin . . . we don't care,
America all . . . ways does its share,
We'll be there with plenty of ammo,
Allies . . . don't ever despair . . .

Baby Doll thought I was a genius. If I was having an especially creative morning she would go running out to the kitchen and bring anyone she could find to hear me.

'Oh, let them begin any warrr . . .' I would be singing, tapping one foot against the fireplace tiles, waving my arms around like a conductor.

Uncle Sam with fight
for the underrr . . . doggg.
Never fear, Allies, never fear.

A new record would drop. Baby Doll would swoop me into her fragrant arms, and we would break into an improvisation on Tommy Dorsey's 'Boogie-Woogie'.

But the Broad Jump Pit would not go away. It loomed in my dreams. If I walked to the store I had to pass the pasture. If I stood on the porch or looked out my grandmother's window, there it was, shimmering in the sunlight, constantly guarded by one of the Olympians.

Things went from bad to worse between me and Dudley. If we so much as passed each other in the hall a fight began. He would hold up his fists and dance around, trying to look like a fighter. When I came flailing at him he would reach underneath my arms and punch me in the stomach.

I considered poisoning him. There was a box of white powder in the toolshed with a skull and crossbones above the label. Several times I took it down and held it in my hands, shuddering at the power it gave me. Only the thought of the electric chair kept me from using it.

Every day Dudley gathered his troops and headed out for the pasture. Every day my hatred grew and festered. Then, just about the time I could stand it no longer, a diversion occurred.

One afternoon about four o'clock an official-looking sedan clattered across the bridge and came roaring down the road to the house.

It was my cousin, Lauralee Manning, wearing her WAVE uniform and smoking Camels in an ivory holder. Lauralee had been widowed at the beginning of the war when her young husband crashed his Navy training plane into the Pacific.

Lauralee dried her tears, joined the WAVES, and went off to avenge his death. I had not seen this paragon since I was a small child, but I had memorized the photograph Miss Onnie Maud, who was Lauralee's mother, kept on her dresser. It was a photograph of Lauralee leaning against the rail of a destroyer.

Not that Lauralee ever went to sea on a destroyer. She was spending the war in Pensacola, Florida, being secretary to an admiral.

Now, out of a clear blue sky, here was Lauralee, home on leave with a two-carat diamond ring and the news that she was getting married.

'You might have called and given some warning,' Miss Onnie Maud said, turning Lauralee into a mass of wrinkles with her embraces. 'You could have softened the blow with a letter.'

'Who's the groom?' my grandmother said. 'I only hope he's not a pilot.'

'Is he an admiral?' I said, 'Or a colonel or a major or a commander?'

'My fiancé's not in uniform, honey,' Lauralee said. 'He's in real estate. He runs the war-bond effort for the whole state of Florida. Last year he collected half a million dollars.'

'In real estate!' Miss Onnie Maud said, gasping. 'What religion is he?'

'He's Unitarian,' she said. 'His name is Donald Marcus.

He's best friends with Admiral Semmes, that's how I met him. And he's coming a week from Saturday, and that's all the time we have to get ready for the wedding.'

'Unitarian!' Miss Onnie Maud said. 'I don't think I've ever met a Unitarian.'

'Why isn't he in uniform?' I insisted.

'He has flat feet,' Lauralee said gaily. 'But you'll love him when you see him.'

Later that afternoon Lauralee took me off by myself for a ride in the sedan.

'Your mother is my favourite cousin,' she said, touching my face with gentle fingers. 'You'll look just like her when you grow up and get your figure.'

I moved closer, admiring the brass buttons on her starched uniform and the brisk way she shifted and braked and put in the clutch and accelerated.

We drove down the river road and out to the bootlegger's shack where Lauralee bought a pint of Jack Daniel's and two Cokes. She poured out half of her Coke, filled it with whisky, and we roared off down the road with the radio playing.

We drove along in the lengthening day. Lauralee was chain-smoking, lighting one Camel after another, tossing the butts out the window, taking sips from her bourbon and Coke. I sat beside her, pretending to smoke a piece of rolled-up paper, making little noises into the mouth of my Coke bottle.

We drove up to a picnic spot on the levee and sat under a tree to look out at the river.

'I miss this old river,' she said. 'When I'm sad I dream about it licking the tops of the levees.'

I didn't know what to say to that. To tell the truth I was afraid to say much of anything to Lauralee. She seemed so splendid. It was enough to be allowed to sit by her on the levee.

'Now, Rhoda,' she said, 'your mother was matron of honour in my wedding to Buddy, and I want you, her own little daughter, to be maid of honour in my second wedding.'

I could hardly believe my ears! While I was trying to think of something to say to this wonderful news I saw that Lauralee was crying, great tears were forming in her blue eyes.

'Under this very tree is where Buddy and I got engaged,' she said. Now the tears were really starting to roll, falling all over the front of her uniform. 'He gave me my ring right where we're sitting.'

'The maid of honour?' I said, patting her on the shoulder, trying to be of some comfort. 'You really mean the maid of honour?'

'Now he's gone from the world,' she continued, 'and I'm marrying a wonderful man, but that doesn't make it any easier. Oh, Rhoda, they never even found his body, never even found his body.'

I was patting her on the head now, afraid she would forget her offer in the midst of her sorrow.

'You mean I get to be the real maid of honour?'

'Oh, yes, Rhoda, honey,' she said. 'The maid of honour, my only attendant.' She blew her nose on a lace-trimmed handkerchief and sat up straighter, taking a drink from the Coke bottle.

'Not only that, but I have decided to let you pick out your own dress. We'll go to Greenville and you can try on every dress at Nell's and Blum's and you can have the one you like the most.'

I threw my arms around her, burning with happiness, smelling her whisky and Camels and the dark Tabu perfume that was her signature. Over her shoulder and through the low branches of the trees the afternoon sun was going down in an orgy of reds and blues and purples and violets, falling from sight, going all the way to China.

Let them keep their nasty Broad Jump Pit, I thought. Wait till they hear about this. Wait till they find out I'm maid of honour in a military wedding.

Finding the dress was another matter. Early the next morning Miss Onnie Maud and my grandmother and Lauralee and I set out for Greenville.

As we passed the pasture I hung out the back window making faces at the athletes. This time they only pretended to ignore me. They couldn't ignore this wedding. It was going to be in the parlour instead of the church so they wouldn't even get to be altar boys. They wouldn't get to light a candle.

'I don't know why you care what's going on in that pasture,' my grandmother said. 'Even if they let you play with them all it would do is make you a lot of ugly muscles.'

'Then you'd have big old ugly arms like Weegie Toler,' Miss Onnie Maud said. 'Lauralee, you remember Weegie Toler, that was a swimmer. Her arms got so big no one would take her to a dance, much less marry her.'

'Well, I don't want to get married anyway,' I said. 'I'm never getting married. I'm going to New York City and be a lawyer.'

'Where does she get those ideas?' Miss Onnie Maud said.

'When you get older you'll want to get married,' Lauralee said. 'Look at how much fun you're having being in my wedding.'

'Well, I'm never getting married,' I said. 'And I'm never having any children. I'm going to New York and be a lawyer and save people from the electric chair.'

'It's the movies,' Miss Onnie Maud said. 'They let her watch anything she likes in Indiana.'

We walked into Nell's and Blum's Department Store and

took up the largest dressing room. My grandmother and Miss Onnie Maud were seated on brocade chairs and every sales lady in the store came crowding around trying to get in on the wedding.

I refused to even consider the dresses they brought from the 'girls' ' department.

'I told her she could wear whatever she wanted,' Lauralee said, 'and I'm keeping my promise.'

'Well, she's not wearing green satin or I'm not coming,' my grandmother said, indicating the dress I had found on a rack and was clutching against me.

'At least let her try it on,' Lauralee said. 'Let her see for herself.' She zipped me into the green satin. It came down to my ankles and fit around my midsection like a girdle, making my waist seem smaller than my stomach. I admired myself in the mirror. It was almost perfect. I looked exactly like a nightclub singer.

'This one's fine,' I said. 'This is the one I want.'

'It looks marvellous, Rhoda,' Lauralee said, 'but it's the wrong colour for the wedding. Remember I'm wearing blue.'

'I believe the child's colour-blind,' Miss Onnie Maud said. 'It runs in her father's family.'

'I am not colour-blind,' I said, reaching behind me and unzipping the dress. 'I have twenty-twenty vision.'

'Let her try on some more,' Lauralee said. 'Let her try on everything in the store.'

I proceeded to do just that, with the sales ladies getting grumpier and grumpier. I tried on a gold gabardine dress with a rhinestone-studded cumberbund. I tried on a pink ballerina-length formal and a lavender voile tea dress and several silk suits. Somehow nothing looked right.

'Maybe we'll have to make her something,' my grandmother said.

'But there's no time,' Miss Onnie Maud said. 'Besides, first we'd have to find out what she wants. Rhoda, please tell us what you're looking for.'

Their faces all turned to mine, waiting for an answer. But I didn't know the answer.

The dress I wanted was a secret. The dress I wanted was dark and tall and thin as a reed. There was a word for what I wanted, a word I had seen in magazines. But what was that word? I could not remember.

'I want something dark,' I said at last. 'Something dark and silky.'

'Wait right there,' the sales lady said. 'Wait just a minute.' Then, from out of a pre-war storage closet she brought a black-watch plaid recital dress with spaghetti straps and a white piqué jacket. It was made of taffeta and rustled when I touched it. There was a label sewn into the collar of the jacket. *Little Miss Sophisticate*, it said. *Sophisticate*, that was the word I was seeking.

I put on the dress and stood triumphant in a sea of ladies and dresses and hangers.

'This is the dress,' I said. 'This is the dress I'm wearing.'

'It's perfect,' Lauralee said. 'Start hemming it up. She'll be the prettiest maid of honour in the whole world.'

All the way home I held the box on my lap thinking about how I would look in the dress. Wait till they see me like this, I was thinking. Wait till they see what I really look like.

I fell in love with the groom. The moment I laid eyes on him I forgot he was flat-footed. He arrived bearing gifts of music and perfume and candy, a warm dark-skinned man with eyes the colour of walnuts.

He laughed out loud when he saw me, standing on the porch with my hands on my hips.

'This must be Rhoda,' he exclaimed, 'the famous red-haired maid of honour.' He came running up the steps, gave me a slow, exciting hug, and presented me with a whole album of Xavier Cugat records. I had never owned a record of my own, much less an album.

Before the evening was over I put on a red formal I found in a trunk and did a South American dance for him to Xavier Cugat's 'Poinciana'. He said he had never seen anything like it in his whole life.

The wedding itself was a disappointment. No one came but the immediate family and there was no aisle to march down and the only music was Onnie Maud playing 'Liebestraum'.

Dudley and Philip and St John and Oliver and Bunky were dressed in long pants and white shirts and ties. They had fresh military crew cuts and looked like a nest of new birds, huddled together on the blue velvet sofa, trying to keep their hands to themselves, trying to figure out how to act at a wedding.

The elderly Episcopal priest read out the ceremony in a gravelly smoker's voice, ruining all the good parts by coughing. He was in a bad mood because Lauralee and Mr Marcus hadn't found time to come to him for marriage instruction.

Still, I got to hold the bride's flowers while he gave her the ring and stood so close to her during the ceremony I could hear her breathing.

The reception was better. People came from all over the Delta. There were tables with candles set up around the porches and sprays of greenery in every corner. There were gentlemen sweating in linen suits and the record player playing every minute. In the back hall Calvin had set up a real professional bar with tall, permanently frosted glasses and ice and mint and lemons and every kind of whisky and liqueur in the world.

I stood in the receiving line getting compliments on my dress, then wandered around the rooms eating cake and letting people hug me. After a while I got bored with that and went out to the back hall and began to fix myself a drink at the bar.

I took one of the frosted glasses and began filling it from different bottles, tasting as I went along. I used plenty of crème de menthe and soon had something that tasted heavenly. I filled the glass with crushed ice, added three straws, and went out to sit on the back steps and cool off.

I was feeling wonderful. A full moon was caught like a kite in the pecan trees across the river. I sipped along on my drink. Then, without planning it, I did something I had never dreamed of doing. I left the porch alone at night. Usually I was in terror of the dark. My grandmother had told me that alligators came out of the bayou to eat children who wander alone at night.

I walked out across the yard, the huge moon giving so much light I almost cast a shadow. When I was nearly to the water's edge I turned and looked back toward the house. It shimmered in the moonlight like a jukebox alive in a meadow, seemed to pulsate with music and laughter and people, beautiful and foreign, not a part of me.

I looked out at the water, then down the road to the pasture. The Broad Jump Pit! There it was, perfect and unguarded. Why had I never thought of doing this before?

I began to run toward the road. I ran as fast as my Mary Jane pumps would allow me. I pulled my dress up around my waist and climbed the fence in one motion, dropping lightly down on the other side. I was sweating heavily, alone with the moon and my wonderful courage.

I knew exactly what to do first. I picked up the pole and hoisted it over my head. It felt solid and balanced and alive. I hoisted it up and down a few times as I had seen Dudley do, getting the feel of it.

Then I laid it ceremoniously down on the ground, reached behind me, and unhooked the plaid formal. I left it lying in a heap on the ground. There I stood, in my cotton underpants, ready to take up pole-vaulting.

I lifted the pole and carried it back to the end of the cinder path. I ran slowly down the path, stuck the pole in the wooden cup, and attempted throwing my body into the air, using it as a lever.

Something was wrong. It was more difficult than it appeared from a distance. I tried again. Nothing happened. I sat down with the pole across my legs to think things over.

Then I remembered something I had watched Dudley doing through the binoculars. He measured down from the end of the pole with his fingers spread wide. That was it, I had to hold it closer to the end.

I tried it again. This time the pole lifted me several feet off the ground. My body sailed across the grass in a neat arc and I landed on my toes. I was a natural!

I do not know how long I was out there, running up and down the cinder path, thrusting my body further and further through space, tossing myself into the pit like a mussel shell thrown across the bayou.

At last I decided I was ready for the real test. I had to vault over a cane barrier. I examined the pegs on the wooden poles and chose one that came up to my shoulder.

I put the barrier pole in place, spit over my left shoulder, and marched back to the end of the path. Suck up your guts, I told myself. It's only a pole. It won't get stuck in your stomach and tear out your insides. It won't kill you.

I stood at the end of the path eyeballing the barrier. Then, above the incessant racket of the crickets, I heard my name being called. Rhoda . . . the voices were calling. Rhoda . . . Rhoda . . . Rhoda . . . Rhoda.

I turned toward the house and saw them coming. Mr Marcus and Dudley and Bunky and Calvin and Lauralee and what looked like half the wedding. They were climbing the fence, calling my name, and coming to get me. Rhoda . . . they called out. Where on earth have you been? What on earth are you doing?

I hoisted the pole up to my shoulders and began to run down the path, running into the light from the moon. I picked up speed, thrust the pole into the cup, and threw myself into the sky, into the still Delta night. I sailed up and was clear and over the barrier.

I let go of the pole and began to fall, which seemed to last a long, long time. It was like falling through clear water. I dropped into the sawdust and lay very still, waiting for them to reach me.

Sometimes I think whatever has happened since has been of no real interest to me.

VICTORY OVER JAPAN

When I was in the third grade I knew a boy who had to have fourteen shots in the stomach as the result of a squirrel bite. Every day at two o'clock they would come to get him. A hush would fall on the room. We would all look down at our desks while he left the room between Mr Harmon and his mother. Mr Harmon was the principal. That's how important Billy Monday's tragedy was.

Mr Harmon came along in case Billy threw a fit. Every day we waited to see if he would throw a fit but he never did. He just put his books away and left the room with his head hanging down on his chest and Mr Harmon and his mother guiding him along between them like a boat.

'Would you go with them like that?' I asked Letitia at recess. Letitia was my best friend. Usually we played girls chase the boys at recess or pushed each other on the swings or hung upside down on the monkey bars so Joe Franke and Bobby Saxacorn could see our underpants but Billy's shots had even taken the fun out of recess. Now we sat around on the fire escape and talked about rabies instead.

'Why don't they put him to sleep first?' Letitia said. 'I'd make them put me to sleep.'

'They can't,' I said. 'They can't put you to sleep unless they operate.'

'My father could,' she said. 'He owns the hospital. He could

72

put me to sleep.' She was always saying things like that but I let her be my best friend anyway.

'They couldn't give them to me,' I said. 'I'd run away to Florida and be a beachcomber.'

'Then you'd get rabies,' Letitia said. 'You'd be foaming at the mouth.'

'I'd take a chance. You don't always get it.' We moved closer together, caught up in the horror of it. I was thinking about the Livingston's bulldog. I'd had some close calls with it lately.

'It was a pet,' Letitia said. 'His brother was keeping it for a pet.'

It was noon recess. Billy Monday was sitting on a bench by the swings. Just sitting there. Not talking to anybody. Waiting for two o'clock, a small washed-out-looking boy that nobody paid any attention to until he got bit. He never talked to anybody. He could hardly even read. When Mrs Jansma asked him to read his head would fall all the way over to the side of his neck. Then he would read a few sentences with her having to tell him half the words. No one would ever have picked him out to be the centre of a rabies tragedy. He was more the type to fall in a well or get sucked down the drain at the swimming pool.

Fourteen days. Fourteen shots. It was spring when it happened and the schoolroom windows were open all day long and every afternoon after Billy left we had milk from little waxy cartons and Mrs Jansma would read us chapters from a wonderful book about some children in England that had a bed that took them places at night. There we were, eating graham crackers and listening to stories while Billy was strapped to the table in Dr Finley's office waiting for his shot.

'I can't stand to think about it,' Letitia said. 'It makes me so sick I could puke.'

'I'm going over there and talk to him right now,' I said. 'I'm going to interview him for the paper.' I had been the only one in the third grade to get anything in the Horace Mann paper. I got in with a story about how Mr Harmon was shell-shocked in the First World War. I was on the lookout for another story that good.

I got up, smoothed down my skirt, walked over to the bench where Billy was sitting and held out a vial of cinnamon toothpicks. 'You want one,' I said. 'Go ahead. She won't care.' It was against the rules to bring cinnamon toothpicks to Horace Mann. They were afraid someone would swallow one.

'I don't think so,' he said. 'I don't need any.'

'Go on,' I said. 'They're really good. They've been soaking all week.'

'I don't want any,' he said.

'You want me to push you on the swings?'

'I don't know,' he said. 'I don't think so.'

'If it was my brother's squirrel, I'd kill it,' I said. 'I'd cut its head off.'

'It got away,' he said. 'It's gone.'

'What's it like when they give them to you?' I said. 'Does it hurt very much?'

'I don't know,' he said. 'I don't look.' His head was starting to slip down onto his chest. He was rolling up like a ball.

'I know how to hypnotize people,' I said. 'You want me to hypnotize you so you can't feel it?'

'I don't know,' he said. He had pulled his legs up on the bench. Now his chin was so far down into his chest I could barely hear him talk. Part of me wanted to give him a shove and see if he would roll. I touched him on the shoulder instead. I could feel his little bones beneath his shirt. I could smell his washed-out rusty smell. His head went all the way down under his knees. Over his shoulder I saw Mrs Jansma headed our way.

'Rhoda,' she called out. 'I need you to clean off the blackboards before we go back in. Will you be a sweet girl and do that for me?'

'I wasn't doing anything but talking to him,' I said. She was beside us now and had gathered him into her wide sleeves. He was starting to cry, making little strangled noises like a goat.

'Well, my goodness, that was nice of you to try to cheer Billy up. Now go see about those blackboards for me, will you?'

I went on in and cleaned off the blackboards and beat the erasers together out the window, watching the chalk dust settle into the bricks. Down below I could see Mrs Jansma still holding on to Billy. He was hanging on to her like a spider but it looked like he had quit crying.

That afternoon a lady from the PTA came to talk to us about the paper drive. 'One more time,' she was saying. 'We've licked the Krauts. Now all we have left is the Japs. Who's going to help?' she shouted.

'I am,' I shouted back. I was the first one on my feet.

'Who do you want for a partner?' she said.

'Billy Monday,' I said, pointing at him. He looked up at me as though I had asked him to swim the English Channel, then his head slid down on the desk.

'All right,' Mrs Jansma said. 'Rhoda Manning and Billy Monday. Team number one. To cover Washington and Sycamore from Calvin Boulevard to Conner Street. Who else?'

'Bobby and me,' Joe Franke called out. He was wearing his coonskin cap, even though it was as hot as summer. How I loved him! 'We want downtown,' he shouted. 'We want Dirkson Street to the river.'

'Done,' Mrs Jansma said. JoEllen Scaggs was writing it all

down on the blackboard. By the time Billy's mother and Mr Harmon came to get him the paper drive was all arranged.

'See you tomorrow,' I called out as Billy left the room. 'Don't forget. Don't be late.'

When I got home that afternoon I told my mother I had volunteered to let Billy be my partner. She was so proud of me she made me some cookies even though I was supposed to be on a diet. I took the cookies and a pillow and climbed up into my tree house to read a book. I was getting to be more like my mother every day. My mother was a saint. She fed hoboes and played the organ at early communion even if she was sick and gave away her ration stamps to anyone that needed them. She had only had one pair of new shoes the whole war.

I was getting more like her every day. I was the only one in the third grade that would have picked Billy Monday to help with a paper drive. He probably couldn't even pick up a stack of papers. He probably couldn't even help pull the wagon.

I bet this is the happiest day of her life, I was thinking. I was lying in my tree house watching her. She was sitting on the back steps putting liquid hose on her legs. She was waiting for the Episcopal minister to come by for a drink. He'd been coming by a lot since my daddy was overseas. That was just like my mother. To be best friends with a minister.

'She picked out a boy that's been sick to help her on the paper drive,' I heard her tell him later. 'I think it helped a lot to get her to lose weight. It was smart of you to see that was the problem.'

'There isn't anything I wouldn't do for you, Ariane,' he said. 'You say the word and I'll be here to do it.'

I got a few more cookies and went back up into the tree house to finish my book. I could read all kinds of books. I could read Book-of-the-Month Club books. The one I was reading now was called *Cakes and Ale*. It wasn't coming along too well.

I settled down with my back against the tree, turning the pages, looking for the good parts. Inside the house my mother was bragging on me. Above my head a golden sun beat down out of a blue sky. All around the silver maple leaves moved in the breeze. I went back to my book. 'She put her arms around my neck and pressed her lips against mine. I forgot my wrath. I only thought of her beauty and her enveloping kindness.

' "You must take me as I am, you know," she whispered.

' "All right," I said.'

Saturday was not going to be a good day for a paper drive. The sky was grey and overcast. By the time we lined up on the Horace Mann playground with our wagons a light rain was falling.

'Our boys are fighting in rain and snow and whatever the heavens send,' Mr Harmon was saying. He was standing on the bleachers wearing an old baseball shirt and a cap. I had never seen him in anything but his grey suit. He looked more shell-shocked than ever in his cap.

'They're working over there. We're working over here. The Germans are defeated. Only the Japs left to go. There're canvas tarps from Gentilly's Hardware, so take one to cover your papers. All right now. One grade at a time. And remember, Mrs Winchester's third grade is still ahead by seventy-eight pounds. So you're going to have to go some to beat that. Get to your stations now. Get ready, get set, go. Everybody working together . . .'

Billy and I started off. I was pulling the wagon, he was walking along beside me. I had meant to wait awhile before I started interviewing him but I started right in.

'Are you going to have to leave to go get it?' I said.

'Go get what?'

'You know. Your shot.'

'I got it this morning. I already had it.'

'Where do they put it in?'

'I don't know,' he said. 'I don't look.'

'Well, you can feel it, can't you?' I said. 'Like, do they stick it in your navel or what?'

'It's higher than that.'

'How long does it take? To get it.'

'I don't know,' he said. 'Till they get through.'

'Well, at least you aren't going to get rabies. At least you won't be foaming at the mouth. I guess you're glad about that.' I had stopped in front of a house and was looking up the path to the door. We had come to the end of Sycamore, where our territory began.

'Are you going to be the one to ask them?' he said.

'Sure,' I said. 'You want to come to the door with me?'

'I'll wait,' he said. 'I'll just wait.'

We filled the wagon by the second block. We took that load back to the school and started out again. On the second trip we hit an attic with bundles of the *Kansas City Star* tied up with string. It took us all afternoon to haul that. Mrs Jansma said she'd never seen anyone as lucky on a paper drive as Billy and I. Our whole class was having a good day. It looked like we might beat everybody, even the sixth grade.

'Let's go out one more time,' Mrs Jansma said. 'One more trip before dark. Be sure and hit all the houses you missed.'

Billy and I started back down Sycamore. It was growing dark. I untied my Brownie Scout sweater from around my waist and put it on and pulled the sleeves down over my wrists. 'Let's try that brick house on the corner,' I said. 'They might be home by now.' It was an old house set back on a high lawn. It looked like a house where old people lived. I had noticed old people were the ones who saved things. 'Come on,' I said. 'You go to the door with me. I'm tired of doing it by myself.'

He came along behind me and we walked up to the door and rang the bell. No one answered for a long time although I could hear footsteps and saw someone pass by a window. I rang the bell again.

A man came to the door. A thin man about my father's age.

'We're collecting paper for Horace Mann School,' I said. 'For the war effort.'

'You got any papers we can have?' Billy said. It was the first time he had spoken to anyone but me all day. 'For the war,' he added.

'There're some things in the basement if you want to go down there and get them,' the man said. He turned a light on in the hall and we followed him into a high-ceilinged foyer with a set of winding stairs going up to another floor. It smelled musty, like my grandmother's house in Clarksville. Billy was right beside me, sticking as close as a burr. We followed the man through the kitchen and down a flight of stairs to the basement.

'You can have whatever you find down here,' he said. 'There're papers and magazines in that corner. Take whatever you can carry.'

There was a large stack of magazines. Magazines were the best thing you could find. They weighed three times as much as newspapers.

'Come on,' I said to Billy. 'Let's fill the wagon. This will put us over the top for sure.' I picked up a bundle and started up the stairs. I went in and out several times carrying as many as I could at a time. On the third trip Billy met me at the foot of the stairs. 'Rhoda,' he said. 'Come here. Come look at this.'

He took me to an old table in a corner of the basement. It

was a walnut table with grapes carved on the side and feet like lion's feet. He laid one of the magazines down on the table and opened it. It was a photograph of a naked little girl, a girl smaller than I was. He turned the page. Two naked boys were standing together with their legs twined. He kept turning the pages. It was all the same. Naked children on every page. I had never seen a naked boy. Much less a photograph of one. Billy looked up at me. He turned another page. Five naked little girls were grouped together around a fountain.

'Let's get out of here,' I said. 'Come on. I'm getting out of here.' I headed for the stairs with him right behind me. We didn't even close the basement door. We didn't even stop to say thank you.

The magazines we had collected were in bundles. About a block from the house we stopped on a corner, breathless from running. 'Let's see if there're any more,' I said. We tore open a bundle. The first magazine had pictures of naked grown people on every page.

'What are we going to do?' he said.

'We're going to throw them away,' I answered, and started throwing them into the nandina bushes by the Hancock's vacant lot. We threw them into the nandina bushes and into the ditch that runs into Mills Creek. We threw the last ones into a culvert and then we took our wagon and got on out of there. At the corner of Sycamore and Wesley we went our separate ways.

'Well, at least you'll have something to think about tomorrow when you get your shot,' I said.

'I guess so,' he replied.

'Look here, Billy. I don't want you to tell anyone about those magazines. You understand?'

'I won't.' His head was going down again.

'I mean it, Billy.'

He raised his head and looked at me as if he had just remembered something he was thinking bout. 'I won't,' he said. 'Are you really going to write about me in the paper?'

'Of course I am. I said I was, didn't I? I'm going to do it tonight.'

I walked on home. Past the corner where the Scout hikes met. Down the alley where I found the card shuffler and the Japanese fan. Past the yard where the violets grew. I was thinking about the boys with their legs twined. They looked like earthworms, all naked like that. They looked like something might fly down and eat them. It made me sick to think about it and I stopped by Mrs Alford's and picked a few iris to take home to my mother.

Billy finished getting his shots. And I wrote the article and of course they put it on page one. BE ON THE LOOKOUT FOR MAD SQUIRREL, the headline read. By Rhoda Katherine Manning. Grade 3.

We didn't even know it was mean, the person it bit said. That person is in the third grade at our school. His name is William Monday. On 23 April he had his last shot. Mrs Jansma's class had a cake and gave him a pencil set. Billy Monday is all right now and things are back to normal.

I think it should be against the law to keep dangerous pets or dogs where they can get out and get people. If you see a dog or squirrel acting funny go in the house and stay there.

I never did get around to telling my mother about those magazines. I kept meaning to but there never seemed to be anywhere to start. One day in August I tried to tell her. I had been to the swimming pool and I thought I saw the man from the brick house drive by in a car. I was pretty sure it was him. As he turned the corner he looked at me. *He looked right at my face*. I stood very still, my heart pounding inside my chest, my hands as cold and wet as a frog, the smell of swimming pool chlorine rising from my skin. What if he found out where I lived? What if he followed me home and killed me to keep me from telling on him? I was terrified. At any moment the car might return. He might grab me and put me in the car and take me off and kill me. I threw my bathing suit and towel down on the sidewalk and started running. I ran down Linden Street and turned into the alley behind Calvin Boulevard, running as fast as I could. I ran down the alley and into my yard and up my steps and into my house looking for my mother to tell her about it.

She was in the living room, with Father Kennimann and Mr and Mrs DuVal. They lived across the street and had a gold star in their window. Warrene, our cook, was there. And Connie Barksdale, our cousin who was visiting from the Delta. Her husband had been killed on Corregidor and she would come up and stay with my mother whenever she couldn't take it any more. They were all in the living room gathered around the radio.

'Momma,' I said. 'I saw this man that gave me some magazines . . .'

'Be quiet, Rhoda,' she said. 'We're listening to the news. Something's happened. We think maybe we've won the war.' There were tears in her eyes. She gave me a little hug, then turned back to the radio. It was a wonderful radio with a magic eye that glowed in the dark. At night when we had blackouts Dudley and I would get into bed with my mother and we would listen to it together, the magic eye glowing in the dark like an emerald.

Now the radio was bringing important news to Seymour, Indiana. Strange, confused, hush-hush news that said we had a bomb bigger than any bomb ever made and we had already dropped it on Japan and half of Japan was sinking into the sea. Now the Japs had to surrender. Now they couldn't come to Indiana and stick bamboo up our fingernails. Now it would all be over and my father would come home.

The grown people kept on listening to the radio, getting up every now and then to get drinks or fix each other sandwiches. Dudley was sitting beside my mother in a white shirt acting like he was twenty years old. He always did that when company came. No one was paying any attention to me.

Finally I went upstairs and lay down on the bed to think things over. My father was coming home. I didn't know how to feel about that. He was always yelling at someone when he was home. He was always yelling at my mother to make me mind.

'What do you mean, you can't catch her,' I could hear him yelling. 'Hit her with a broom. Hit her with a table. Hit her with a chair. But, for God's sake, Ariane, don't let her talk to you that way.'

Well, maybe it would take a while for him to get home. First they had to finish off Japan. First they had to sink the other half into the sea. I curled up in my soft old eiderdown comforter. I was feeling great. We had dropped the biggest bomb in the world on Japan and there were plenty more where that one came from.

I fell asleep in the hot sweaty silkiness of the comforter. I was dreaming I was at the wheel of an airplane carrying the bomb to Japan. Hit 'em, I was yelling. Hit 'em with a mountain. Hit 'em with a table. Hit 'em with a chair. Off we go into the wild blue yonder, climbing high into the sky. I dropped one on the brick house where the bad man lived, then took off for Japan. Down we dive, spouting a flame from under. Off with one hell of a roar. We live in flame. Buckle down in flame. For nothing can stop the Army Air Corps. Hit 'em with a table, I was yelling. Hit 'em with a broom. Hit 'em with a bomb. Hit 'em with a chair.

THE GAUZY EDGE OF PARADISE

The only reason Lanier and I went to the coast to begin with was to lose weight. We didn't know we were going to have a *ménage à trois* with Sandor. We didn't even know Sandor was coming down there.

Lanier and I are best friends. We've been going on diets together since we were thirteen years old. We dieted together through high school and Ole Miss and when we went to Jackson to be secretaries to the legislature. That's what we do now. Lanier's secretary to Senator Huddleston from Bovina and I'm secretary to Senator Ladd from Aberdeen. It's good work but you're sitting down all day. The fat settles. I'm not giving in to that. 'It's natural,' my mother says. 'You're too hard on yourself, Diane. Let nature have some say.'

'Not on my hips,' I tell her. 'I'll die before I'll get fat. I'll jump off a bridge. You forget, Mother, I'm not married yet.'

'Whose fault is that?' she says. 'Certainly not the young men you've left crying in the living room. The rings you've returned. Not to mention Fanny Claiborne's son.' It's true. I've broken three engagements. Something just comes over me. Suddenly I look at them and they look so pitiful, the way their hands start to look like paws.

Meanwhile the problem is to keep my body going uphill. I'm twenty-nine this August. I've got to watch it. Well, I've got Lanier. And she's got me or she would have given in long ago. She'd be the size of a house if I didn't keep after her.

*

This trip to the coast was a Major Diet. We'd been at it five days, taking Escatrol, reading poetry out loud to keep ourselves in a spiritual frame of mind, exercising morning, night and noon. I was down to 126 and Lanier was down to 129 when Mother called and asked us to pick up Sandor in Pensacola. 'Try to keep him from drinking,' she said. 'Aunt Treena and Uncle Lamar are worried sick about him drinking. And be on time, Diane. There's nothing worse than getting off a plane and no one's there. Are you listening? Diane, are you listening to me?'

I was listening. I was leaning against the portable dishwasher wondering what effect Sandor's coming would have on our diet. A diet's a very delicate thing. You have to keep your momentum going. You have to stick to your routine. Well, it was Mother's beach house, and if she told Sandor he could come there was nothing I could do but meet the plane.

'Who's coming?' Lanier said. 'Who's on their way?'

'My cousin, this gorgeous cousin of mine that had a nervous breakdown trying to be a movie star. He used to be a football player before he took up acting. Then he went to California. He's got these beautiful shoulders and he plays a saxophone. Haven't you ever been here when he was here?'

She was pulling on her leotards. We wear them even in the heat. To make us sweat. There are several schools of thought about that. Lanier and I are of the school that says the hotter you get the better. 'Let's don't take a pill today if we're going to Pensacola,' she said. 'I'm sick of taking them. They make me nervous. They make me talk too much.'

'We have to take them. Ten days. Ten pills. We swore we'd do it. Besides, I'd take cyanide to get this fat off my stomach.' I handed her a pill and a glass of water. 'Come on. Just four more days. Go on. Take it. Then we'll do leg raises, then stomach crunches, then we'll run down to the beach and take a swim. You have to look on this as a religious experience, Lanier. Pretend you're the Buddha going on a fast. Or Jesus in the wilderness or something.'

She took it and put it in her mouth and swallowed it. We had gone to a lot of trouble to get that Escatrol. We had begged a young surgeon for weeks, convincing him we wouldn't tell where we got it. Or drink on top of it.

She put down the water glass and heaved a sigh. Lanier's got a lot of guilt. She can even feel guilty about going on a fast. I work on her and work on her but she's still that way. 'OK,' she said. 'I want to try standing in the waves for an hour again. I could tell a big difference in my thighs today. I think they look a lot better.' She took the aerobic dance record out of its cover and put it on the turntable. 'What's he like, this Sandor?'

'He's sad,' I said. 'Beautiful and sad. Even when he plays his saxophone it's always sad music, songs he writes. If you ask him to play anything you know he puts it back in the case. Anyway, he's gorgeous. If worse comes to worse we can always look at him.'

'Let's start on the exercises. I think the pill's taking effect. I'm starting to feel it. I'm going to try to get in my pink denim skirt to wear to Pensacola.' She dropped the needle down on the record and we went into our routine.

'Get those bodies working,' a woman named Joanie demanded. 'Let's see some action if you want attraction. He's not going to love you if he has that fat stomach to contend with. You can't hide beneath an overblouse for ever. Come on,' she was getting mean now. 'You grew it. You lift it. Squeeze it. Squeeze it like you mean it. Squeeze it like you own it . . .'

We bent and stretched, jumped and pulled, turned and squeezed, panted and breathed, groaned and creaked.

'Stretch those old traps,' Joanie demanded. 'How long since you felt a good stretch in the old pecs? Crunch it. Crunch it like you mean it. Feel that stuff melting. The fat's on the fire . . .'

We finished up with a hundred jumping jacks and fell back on the floor exhausted.

'Your midriff looks a lot better,' Lanier said. 'I swear I can see your ribs.'

'You think so?' I walked over to Momma's gilt picture frame mirror and surveyed my ribs. 'Oh, God, if they would only show from the back. If only once more before I died I could see the ribs in my back. The last time was that year I was engaged to Saint-John Royals. Remember that year? I weighed 114 for five straight months.' I gazed off into a découpage umbrella stand, glorying in the memory. 'Maybe I should have married him.'

'I think it's time for us to marry someone,' Lanier said. 'I think we're going to have to lower our standards, Diane. He's really gorgeous, your cousin Sandor?'

'Like a god. I don't know why he didn't go over in Hollywood. I guess the sadness showed up on the screen test.'

'What's he sad about?'

'I don't know. It's just how he is. He's always been that way.'

'Maybe we can fix him up,' she said, and laughed her old skit night laugh. Lanier's a riot when she wants to be. 'Maybe we can cheer old Sandor up.' She settled her hands on her hips and gazed out the window at the water.

We were in my mother's beach house, a frame house up on stilts, looking out on the Gulf of Mexico at the exact point where the state of Alabama meets the state of Florida. A dark green house with white shutters. White sand stretching as far as the eye can see, clean white dunes and deep green sea and always a breeze even on the hottest day. The Redneck Riviera people call that part of the country now, rednecks and power boats and waterfront developments growing up beside every little stagnant bayou. Baldwin County, Alabama. Black man, don't let the sun go down on you. The natives used to boast there wasn't a black man in the county limits. The white people have these opaque blue eyes. Churches on every corner. A man who boasts he can kill, pluck, cook and eat a chicken in eighty seconds.

Still, I loved it. I'd been going down there all my life. From a time when it was so desolate you had to stop in Mobile for groceries. When we hauled drinking water from behind the Orange Beach post office. When the dolphins still swam by the pier in the mornings, lifting their heads to look at us, rolling and playing, touching and caressing, nudging each other with their snouts. 'Why would you need to read a book about dolphins to know how smart they are?' my mother said to me one day. 'Anybody that ever saw one could figure that out.'

Lanier and I finished up our morning routine and dressed and got into the car. We had a cooler with some Tabs and carrot sticks and shredded cabbage and one small apple apiece. Not that we were hungry. Escatrol takes care of being hungry.

We were feeling good. Lanier had made it into the pink skirt and I was wearing a yellow playsuit, *with a belt*. We stopped at a gift shop in Gulf Shores and found some cards to send to Jackson and had our picture taken together in a three-for-a-dollar photograph machine. We always did that when we came to the coast. It was part of our history. Then we went into the Gulf Shores doughnut shop to look at the buckets of lemon filling that were always sitting on the floor with flies all over them and the tops half off. Aversion therapy. Lanier's the one that thought that up. It still worked. They hadn't changed management and cleaned it up.

At the drugstore Lanier bought a book about Anita Bryant's private life and read it out loud to me all the way to Pensacola, putting in the stuff the writer left out. 'Anita Bryant was always very close to her father, Big Jack Bryant,' the book would say. 'Oh, Big Jack, show me again that big black secret thing of yours,' Lanier would add. We thought it was hilarious. We laughed all the way to Pensacola. Escatrol, queen of prescription drugs.

Sandor looked wonderful getting off the plane. He didn't look like he'd had a nervous breakdown. He didn't even look as sad as usual. He had on a beige shirt with epaulets, made of some soft material. And tan slacks with no belt. This Greek god kind of blond hair, with natural streaks. I couldn't believe I'd been sorry a minute that he was coming. Lanier went crazy when she saw him. You could hear her pull her stomach in.

She moved right in. 'You want an Escatrol,' she said. We were waiting for the luggage. She'd forgotten I was there. 'Diane and I have some Escatrol. We got it from a doctor. You want one? You can have one if you want it.' 'Sure,' he said. 'Where are they?' She took the bottle out of her purse. We'd been taking turns keeping them. She undid the safety cap, took out a green and white capsule and held it out to him. 'Happy landings,' she said. They laughed like old buddies. Sandor took the pill from her and walked off toward the water fountain.

'Let's have a party,' he said when he got back. 'Where do you want to start?'

We started at this place called the Quarter, modelled on the

French Quarter in New Orleans. Six different bars under one roof. Every bar has a different kind of music, juke boxes in the daytime, live bands at night. Country music in one place, jazz guitar in the next, rock and roll, new wave. One even has old fifties stuff, for old people, so they can hear their old songs.

It was four in the afternoon when we got there. Everything was just getting started for the night. The bartenders changing shifts, people wiping off the tables, straightening chairs, dusting glasses. We started in a part called the Seven Sailors. Fishnets on the wall and stuffed monkeys and parrots hanging from the nets and a juke box with Greek music. Sandor ordered a double gin martini and Lanier ordered wine and somehow or other I decided on a Salty Dog. Tequila on top of dexadrine is sort of like you took sunlight and squeezed it through a cylinder so what comes out the other end is the size of a thread. The thread is how you feel for about thirty minutes. After that, well, there's good and bad in everything. You have to take your chances, make your choices. Not that we were making the right ones that day. Only I'm not going to start feeling guilty about it. Even with what happened next. Even if I'll see him standing in that door holding a gun for ever. Even if I'll feel his hands on my arms till the day I die.

We settled down at a table with our drinks. 'I heard you had a nervous breakdown,' I said, moving my chair over close to Sandor's.

'Who told you that?' he said.

'Momma said Aunt Treena said so. Well, did you have one or not?'

'No, I didn't have a nervous breakdown. I checked into a hospital because Hollywood was driving me crazy. I needed to think things over. It was a good rest. I decided the best thing to do was come on home and settle down and get a regular job. So here I am.' He smiled that gorgeous smile and took a big drink of his martini. 'That's dynamite speed. Where did you get it? You can't get stuff like that even on the Coast.'

'It's for a diet,' I said. 'We had to take the prescription to five drugstores to get it filled. They don't even stock it anymore. Lanier and I are going to be so thin when we get back to Jackson no one will even know us. What kind of job are you going to get?'

'I don't know. Whatever they'll let me do. Selling cars or construction work. Maybe real estate. I'm not worried. I'll think of something. Something'll turn up.'

'Of course you're worried,' I said. 'You're worried sick. You've wasted your youth trying to be a movie star and now you haven't got a profession. Don't try to pretend you aren't worried about that, Sandor.'

'I guess you're right,' he said. 'I guess I'm more worried than I realize.'

'Come up to Jackson where we are,' Lanier said. 'There's always work around the legislature. Senator Huddleston will find you something.'

'That's an idea,' he said. 'Maybe I'll drive up with you when you leave.' He signalled the waiter and we had another round of drinks. Then I got an idea. 'Let's rent a hotel room and park the car and take taxis and go on and get good and drunk,' I said. 'Let's celebrate Sandor returning to Dixie. Back in the fold. No Tails. That's what we called Sandor when he was little, Lanier. One summer we were all at the beach house and he discovered he didn't have a tail. He was just a little boy. He'd go around all summer pointing out his back end to people. No tails, he'd say. No tails.'

'That's the trouble with getting drunk with your cousins,' Sandor said. 'They tell everything you did. We called Diane the Duchess because she always tried to boss everyone around.'

'She's still that way,' Lanier said. Now they had that in common. I had tried to boss them both around. She leaned against his arm. Sandor was leaning back. They were leaning on each other. But what about me? Who was I supposed to lean on?

We found a taxi and went over to the old Piedmont Hotel and got a room and took a shower and put our clothes back on and went out and got drunker. On the way out of the room I took one of the Escatrol capsules and opened it up on a piece of hotel stationery and we took turns licking up the little green and yellow balls with our tongues. 'Why not,' I said to Sandor. It was an old thing my cousins and I like to say when we're really going to get in trouble. 'Whyyyyyyy not,' he answered.

Around ten that night we ended up at a gay bar called the Monkey's Paw listening to a female impersonator named Lady Aurelius. She was singing Barbra Streisand when we came in. People, people who need people. Songs like that. It made me feel like crying. I sat there watching Lady Aurelius mouthing the words of a Barbra Streisand album, missing all my old boyfriends and fiancés. Some day he'll come along, Lady Aurelius was singing now, switching styles. *The man I love.*

I don't know what came over me. I'm not an exhibitionist. Maybe I was sick of watching Sandor and Lanier lean on each other. Maybe I was under the influence of the Monkey's Paw. All those smiling faces. I got up and walked up on the stage and went over to Lady Aurelius and put my arm around her waist and started helping her sing. 'I've got to be me,' I was singing. 'I've got to be me.' I was into it. I moved out in front of her. I took the stage. She didn't seem to mind. She was a very strong looking female impersonator. As tall as my father. I started screaming out new words to the songs. *I've got to be me. No matter what happens. Or how much it hurts anybody. Or whether they like it or not. To hell with it. I've got to be me. I've got to be me.*

I was right up to the edge of the stage yelling my head off. Then I started doing my exercise routine. Rolling my arms around in the air, bending from side to side so the audience could see how supple I was. Twisting and shaking and doing the boogie. I looked back at Lady Aurelius. She had stopped smiling. She was standing very still.

Someone in the audience started throwing money. A handful of change hit the stage. Some dollar bills. A wad of paper. More change. A paper cup. I was yelling out more words. Anything I thought up. Now I wasn't even bothering with the music. *Anybody that wants to stop me has got another think coming*, I sang. *Diane doesn't stop for no man. No man calls my name. No man's got the drop on me. No one's got my number*. About like that.

I could see it all so clearly. I had missed my calling. I was a singer who had never gotten to sing. A singer who forgot to sing. I had been denied my destiny. I meant to stay up there all night and make up for lost time but a bouncer came up on the stage and dragged me off and delivered me to Sandor.

After that the heart went out of the evening. The bars were closing. The streets looking wet and deserted. We wandered back to the Quarter to see if we could recapture the night but the night was gone. The parrots were falling from the nets, someone had turned a pitcher of beer over on a table. It was dripping slowly down off the black leather edges. My mind kept going away. I kept thinking about fields of wheat I had seen once in Kansas. Fields of barley. Malt growing somewhere I had never visited. Rain falling. All of that to end up beer. A surly, embarrassing fat sort of drink.

We piled into a taxi and told the driver to take us home. It was some off-brand taxi company. The driver was a hard-looking black man without much to say. He didn't turn his head until we got to the hotel. Then Sandor pulled a wad of money out of his pocket to pay him and half of it fell on the floor and we had to pick it up. We were too drunk to tell the ones from the tens. Finally Sandor handed the driver a handful and we got out and went on up to our room.

It was Lanier who thought up the *ménage à trois*. I guess she didn't want me to feel left out. I was so depressed by then I'd have gone along with anything. We took off our clothes and got in bed and started trying to decide what to do. I couldn't find anything I really wanted to do. Finally I ended up with my mouth on Sandor's arm, sort of sucking on his arm. Sandor and Lanier kept kissing each other, stopping every now and then to try to kiss me or pat me here or there. 'Stop it, Lanier,' I said finally. 'I may be crazy but so far I'm not queer.'

'This isn't queer,' she said. 'It's a *ménage à trois*. Everyone in Paris used to do this. I read about it in a book by Simone, what's her name. You're the one that always wants to be so free, Diane.'

I sighed. Sandor rubbed his hand across my head. I patted him on the back and tried to roll over to the unused part of the bed. I knew we should have gotten two rooms, I was thinking. But I can't sleep by myself in a hotel. I never sleep a wink.

'Come on, Diane,' Sandor said in his sweetest voice. 'Let me make you feel good too. Come back over here by me.' I was going to do it but I heard a sound, like breathing underwater. I looked toward the door. The black man was standing in the door with a gun in his hand. He moved into the room and closed the door. He had a face like a shell. We were all very still. We had been waiting all our lives for this to happen. Now it was here.

'One of you get out of bed and collect the money for me,' he said. 'Come on. I'm sick of all this shit. I'd just as soon shoot all three of you in the face as look at you. Come on. Come on. And if you turn me in to the police I'll track you down and have your asses. So think it over before you file a report.'

Lanier got out of the bed. She was trying to tie the sheet around her but it was still attached at the bottom of the bed. She picked up her pants to put them on then thought better of that and started sort of skipping or hopping around the room getting our billfolds. She laid everything she could find on the untouched bed. Sandor and I were very still. I don't know what we were doing. 'That's it,' the man said. 'Now take the driver's licenses and credit cards out of the billfolds and the money and any jewellery you have. Come over here. Put them on the floor. About a foot from me. That's it. That's a good girl. You sure are a big girl to have such little tiny teats. That's it. Now then, go tie your buddies up. Tear off part of the sheet and tie their hands behind them. On the bed. Come on. Hurry up. I'm sick of all this shit. I'd just as soon kill all three of you. Save tying you up.'

'I'll tie them up as fast as I can,' Lanier said. 'I used to be a Girl Scout. I know how to tie things.' I couldn't believe how cool she was being. Like she had forgotten she was naked. 'We have some Escatrol,' she said. 'It's a prescription drug. It's very hard to get. Would you like that too? It's in my pocketbook. Should I get that and put it by the money?'

'Yeah,' he said. 'I'll take it. Put it there, pancake teats, then get on that bed. I'll do the tying.' He was wearing a dark jacket with a white shirt. That's all I remember. Except his face, like an oyster shell. There was a design on the shirt, calligraphy. In black and red. Lanier walked right over to him and laid the stuff on the floor. I thought he would hit her with the gun but he let her go away. Then he tied her to the other bed and cut

the phone wires and tied our hands together. I closed my eyes
when he touched me. His hands were so cold. I will feel them
until I die. He turned off all the lights and left the room.

Everything was very quiet when we got back to Momma's
house the next afternoon. The beaches were deserted as far as
I could see. Hardly a seagull was in sight. I went into the
kitchen and started making chocolate milkshakes with some
old mouldy ice cream I found in the freezer. I made them so
thick you had to eat them with a spoon. I ate half a pound of
ice cream while I was getting them ready. I took one and gave
it to Sandor. He was lying on the living room floor watching
TV. I took one to Lanier. She was on the sleeping porch
reading a magazine. I took mine and a bag of chocolate mint
cookies and went into my mother's bedroom and lay down on
the bed and started nibbling on the cookies. It was six o'clock.
Before long it would be seven o'clock. Then it would be night.
The old heron by the pier would snuggle down into his nest.
All my life I had wondered where he put his feet. I pulled my
knees up against my soft full stomach. I would never weigh
114 again as long as I lived. Nothing would change. Good girls
would press their elegant rib cages against their beautiful rich
athletic husbands. Passionate embraces would ensue. I would
be lying on a bed drinking chocolate milkshakes. Eating
cookies. Wishing Lanier hadn't given the Escatrol away.

THE DOUBLE HAPPINESS BUN

Nora Jane Whittington was going to have a baby. There was no getting around that. First Freddy Harwood talked her into taking out her Lippes Loop. 'I don't like the idea of a piece of copper stuck up your vagina,' he said. 'I think you ought to get it out.'

'It's not in my vagina. It's in my womb. And it's real small. I saw it before they put it in.'

'How small?' he said. 'Let me see.' Nora Jane held up a thumb and forefinger and made a circle. 'Like this,' she said. 'About like this.'

'Hmmmmmmmmm . . .' he said, and let it go at that. But the idea was planted. She kept thinking about the little piece of copper. How it resembled a mosquito coil. Like shrapnel, she thought. Like having some kind of weapon in me. Nora Jane had a very good imagination for things like that. Finally imagination won out over science and she called the obstetrician and made an appointment. There was really not much to it. She lay down on the table and squeezed her eyes shut and the doctor reached up inside her with a small cold instrument and the Lippes Loop came sliding out.

'Now what will you do?' the doctor said. 'Would you like me to start you on the pill?'

'Not yet,' she said. 'Let me think it over for a while.'

'Don't wait too long,' he said. 'You're a healthy girl. It can happen very quickly.'

'All right,' she said. 'I won't.' She gathered up her things and drove on over to Freddy's house to cook things in his gorgeous redwood kitchen.

'Now what will we do?' she said. 'You think I ought to take the pill? Or what?' It was much later that evening. Nora Jane was sitting on the edge of the hot tub looking up at the banks of clouds passing before the moon. It was one of those paradisial San Francisco nights, flowers and pine trees, eucalyptus and white wine and Danish bread and brie.

Nora Jane's legs were in the hot tub. Her back was to the breeze coming from the bay. She was wearing a red playsuit with a red and yellow scarf tied around her forehead like a flag. Freddy Harwood thought she was the most desirable thing he had ever seen in his whole life.

'We'll think of something,' he said. He took off his Camp Pericles senior counsellor camp shorts and lowered himself into the water. He was thirty-five years old and every summer he still packed his footlocker full of T-shirts and flashlight batteries and went off to the Adirondacks to be a counsellor in his old camp. That's how crazy he was. The rest of the year he ran a bookstore in Berkeley.

'What do you think we'll think of?' she said, joining him in the water, sinking down until the ends of the scarf floated in the artificial waves. What they thought of lasted half the night and moved from the hot tub to the den floor to the bedroom. Freddy Harwood thought it was the most meaningful evening he had spent since the night he lost his cherry to his mother's best friend. Nora Jane didn't think it was all that great. It lacked danger, that aphrodisiac, that sugar to end all sugars.

'We have to get married,' he told her in the morning. 'You'll have to marry me. He walked around a ladder and picked up a kimono and pulled it on and tied the belt into a bowline. The ladder was the only furniture in the room except the bed they had been sleeping in. Freddy was in the process of turning his bedroom into a planetarium. He was putting the universe on the ceiling, little dots of heat-absorbing cotton that glowed in the night like stars. Each dot had to be measured with long paper measuring strips from the four corners of the room. It was taking a lot longer to put the universe on the ceiling than Freddy had thought it would. He turned his eyes to a spot he had reserved for Altabaron. It was the summer sky he was re-creating, as seen from Minneapolis where the kits were made. 'Yes,' he said, as if he were talking to himself. 'We are going to have to get married.'

'I don't want to get married,' she said. 'I'm not in love with you.'

'You are in love with me. You just don't know it yet.'

'I am not in love with you. I've never told you that I was. Besides, I wouldn't want to change my name. Nora Harwood, how would that sound?'

'How could you make love to someone like last night if you didn't love them? I don't believe it.'

'I don't know. I guess I'm weird or abnormal or something. But I know whether I'm in love with someone or not. Anyway, I like you better than anyone I've met in San Francisco. I've told you that.' She was getting dressed now, pulling a white cotton sweater over a green cotton skirt, starting to look even more marvellous than she did with no clothes on at all. Freddy sighed, gathered his forces, walked across the room and took her in his arms. 'Do you want to have a priest? Or would you settle for a judge. I have this friend that's a federal judge who would love to marry us.'

'I'm not marrying you, Freddy. Not for all the tea in China. Not even for your money and I want you to stop being in love with me. I want you to be my friend and have fun like we used to. Now listen, do you want me to give you back that car you gave me? I'll give you back the car.'

'Please don't give me back the car. All my life I wanted to give someone a blue convertible. Don't ruin it by talking like that.'

'I'm sorry. That was mean of me. I knew better than to say that. I'll keep that car for ever. You know that. I might get buried in that car.' She gave him a kiss on his freckled chest, tied a green scarf around her hair, floated out of the house, got into the blue convertible and away she went, weaving in and out of the lanes of traffic, thinking about how hard it was to find out what you wanted in the world, much less what to do to get it.

It was either that night that fertilized one of Nora Jane Whittington's wonderful, never to be replaced or duplicated as long as the species lasts, small, wet, murky, secret-bearing eggs. Or it was two nights later when she heard a love song coming out of an open doorway and broke down and called Sandy Halter and he came and got her and they went off to a motel and made each other cry.

Sandy was the boy Nora Jane had lived with in New Orleans. She had come to California to be with him but there was a mix-up and he didn't meet her plane. Then she found out he'd been seeing a girl named Pam. After that she couldn't love him anymore. Nora Jane was very practical about love. She only loved people that loved her back. She never was sure what made her call up Sandy that night in Berkeley. First she dreamed about him. Then she passed a doorway and heard Bob Dylan singing. 'Lay, lady, lay. Lay across my big brass bed.' The next thing she knew she was in a motel room making love and crying. Nora Jane was only practical about love most of the time. Part of the time she was just as dumb about it as everybody else in the world.

'How can we make up?' she said, sitting up in the rented bed. 'After what you did to me.'

'We can't help making up. We love each other. I've got some big things going on, Nora Jane. I want you working with me. It's real money this time. Big money.' He sat up beside her and put his hands on his knees. He looked wonderful. She had to admit that. He was as tan as an Indian and his hair was as blond as sunlight and his mind as faraway and unavailable as a star.

'Last night I dreamed about you,' she said. 'That's why I called you up. It was raining like crazy in my dream and we were back in New Orleans, on Magazine Street, looking out the window, and the trees were blowing all over the place, and I said, Sandy, there's going to be a hurricane. Let's turn on the radio. And you said, no, the best thing to do is go to the park and ride it out in a live oak tree. Then we went out on to the street. It was a dream, remember, and Webster Street and Henry Clay were under water and they were trying to get patients out of the Home for the Incurables. They were bringing them out on stretchers. It was awful. It was raining so hard. Then I got separated from you. I was standing in the door of the Webster Street Bar calling to you and no one was coming and the water was rising. It was a terrible dream. Then you were down the street with that girl. I guess it was her. She was blond and sort of fat and she was holding on to you. Pam, I guess it was Pam.'

'I haven't seen Pam since all that happened. Pam doesn't mean a thing to me. Pam's nothing.'

'Then why was I dreaming about her?'

'Don't ruin everything, Nora Jane. Let's just love each other.'

'You want to make love to me some more? Well, do you?'

'No, right now I want a cigarette. Then I want to take you to this restaurant I like. I want to tell you about this outfit I'm working for. I'll tell you what. Tomorrow's Saturday and I have to take Mirium's car back so I'll take you with me and show you what's going on.'

'I've been wondering what you were up to.'

'Just wait till you meet Mirium. She's my boss. I've told her all about you. Now come on, let's get dressed and get some dinner. I haven't eaten all day.' Sandy had gotten out of bed and was putting on his clothes. White linen pants and a blue shirt with long full sleeves. He liked to dress up even more than Nora Jane did.

Sandy's boss, Mirium Sallisaw, was forty-three years old. She lived in a house on a bluff overlooking the sea between Pacifica and Montara. It was a very expensive house she bought with money she made arranging trips to Mexico for people that wanted to cure cancer with Laetrile. The Laetrile market was dying out but Mirium wasn't worried. She was getting into Interferon as fast as she could make the right connections. Interferon and Energy. Those were Mirium's key words for 1983.

'Energy,' she was fond of saying. 'Energy. That's all. There's nothing else.' She imagined herself as a little glowworm in a sea of dark branches, spreading light to the whole forest. She was using Sandy to keep her batteries charged. She liked to get in bed with him at night and charge up, then tell him her theories about energy and how he could have all the other women he wanted, because she, Mirium Sallisaw, was above human jealousy and didn't care. Sandy was only

103

twenty-two years old. He believed everything she told him. He even believed she was dying to meet Nora Jane. He thought of Mirium as this brilliant businesswoman who would jump at a chance to have someone as smart as Nora Jane help drive patients back and forth across the border.

Nora Jane and Sandy got to Mirium's house late in the afternoon. They parked in the parking lot and walked across a lawn with Greek statues set here and there as if the decorator hadn't been able to decide where they should go. Statues of muses faced the parking lot. Statues of heroes looked out upon the sea. Twin statues of cupid guarded the doorway.

Nora Jane and Sandy opened the door and stepped into the foyer. It was dark inside the house. All the drapes were closed. The only light came from recessed fixtures near the ceiling. A young man in a silk shirt and elegant pointed shoes came walking toward them. 'Hello, Sandy,' he said. 'Mother's in the back. Go tell her you're here.'

'This is Maurice,' Sandy said. 'He's Mirium's son. He's a genius, aren't you, Maurice? Listen, did you give Mirium my message? Does she know Nora Jane's coming?'

'We've got dinner reservations at Blanchard's. They have fresh salmon. Mimi called. Do you like salmon?' he said to Nora Jane. 'I worship it. It's all I eat.'

'I've never given it much thought,' she said. 'I don't think much about what I eat.'

'Maurice takes chemistry courses at the college,' Sandy said. 'Mirium's making him into a chemist.'

'That's nice,' she said. 'That must be interesting.'

'Well, profitable. I'll make some dough if I stick to it. Sandy, why don't you go back and tell her you're here. She's in the exercise room with Mimi. Tell her I'm getting hungry.' Sandy disappeared down a long hall.

Maurice took Nora Jane into a sunken living room with sofas arranged around a marble coffee table. There were oriental boxes on the table and something that looked like a fire extinguisher.

'Sit down,' he said. 'I'll play you some music. I've got a new tape some friends of mine made. It's going to be big. Warner's has it and Twentieth Century–Fox is interested. Million Bucks, that's the name of the group. The leader's name is Million Bills. No kidding, he had it changed. Listen to this.'

Maurice pushed some buttons on the side of the marble table and the music came on, awful erratic music, a harp and a lot of electronic keyboards and guitars and synthesizers. The harp would play a few notes, then the electrical instruments would shout it down.

'Pretty chemical, huh? Feel that energy? They're going to be big.' He was staring off into the recessed light, one hand on the emerald embedded in his ear.

Nora Jane couldn't think of anything to say. She settled back into the sofa cushions. It was cool and dark in the room. The cushions she was leaning into were the softest things she had ever felt in her life. They felt alive, like some sort of hair. She reached her hands behind her. 'What are these cushions?' she said. 'What are they made of?'

'They're Mirium's old fur coats. She wanted drapes but there wasn't enough.'

'They're made of fur coats?'

'Yeah. Before that they were animals. Crazy, huh? Chemical? Look, if you want a joint, there're different kinds in those boxes. That red one's Colombian and the blue one is some stuff we're getting from Arkansas. Heavy. Really heavy. There's gas in the canister if you'd rather have that. I quit doing it. Too sweet for me. I don't like a sweet taste.'

'Could I have a glass of water?' she said. 'It was a long drive.' She was sitting up, trying not to touch the cushions.

'Sure,' he said. 'I'll get you some. Just a minute.' He had taken a tube of something out of his pocket and was applying it to his lips.

'This is a new gloss. It's dynamite. Mint and lemon mixed together. Wild!'

Then, so quickly Nora Jane didn't have time to resist, Maurice sat down beside her and put his mouth on hers. He was very strong for a boy who looked so thin and he was pressing her down into the fur pillows. Her mouth was full of the taste of mint and lemon and something tingly, like an anaesthetic. For a moment she thought he was trying to kill her. 'Get off of me,' she said. She pushed against him with all her might. He sat up and looked away. 'I just wanted you to get the full effect.'

'How old are you?'

'Sixteen. Isn't it a drag?'

'I don't know. I'd never have guessed you were a day over four. Three or four.'

'I guess it's my new stylist,' he said, as if he didn't know what she meant. 'I've got this woman in Marin. Marilee at Plato's. It takes for ever to get there. But it's worth it. I mean, that woman understands hair . . .'

Sandy reappeared with a woman wearing grey slacks and a dark sweater. She looked as if she smiled about once a year. She held out her hand, keeping the other one on Sandy's arm. 'Well,' she said. 'We've been hearing about you. Sandy's told us all about your exploits together in New Orleans. He says you can do some impressive tricks with your voice. How about letting us hear some?'

'I don't do tricks,' Nora Jane said. 'I don't even sing any more.'

'Well, I guess that's that. Did Sandy fill you in on the operation we've got going down here? It isn't illegal, you know. But I don't like our business mouthed around. Too many jealous people, if you know what I mean.'

'He told me some things . . .' Nora Jane looked at Sandy. He wouldn't meet her eyes. He picked up one of the canisters and took out a joint and lit it and passed it to Maurice.

'We have dinner reservations in less than an hour,' Mirium said. 'Let's have some wine, then get going. I can't stand to be late and lose our table. Maurice, try that buzzer. See if you can get someone in here.'

'These are sick people you send places,' Nora Jane said. 'That you need a driver for?'

'Oh, honey, they're worse than sick. These people are at the end. I mean, the end. We're the last chance they've got.'

'They don't care what it costs,' Sandy said. 'They pay in cash.'

'So what does it do for them?' Nora Jane said. 'Does it make them well?'

'It makes them happy,' Maurice said.

'It makes them better than they were,' Mirium said. 'If they have faith. It won't work without faith. Faith makes the energy start flowing. You see, honey, the real value of Laetrile is it gets the energy flowing. Right, Sandy?' She moved over beside him and took the joint from between his fingers. 'Like good sex. It keeps the pipes open, if you know what I mean.' She put her hand on Sandy's sleeves, caressing his sleeve.

'Do you have a powder room?' Nora Jane said. 'A bathroom, I mean?'

'There's one in the foyer,' Miriam said. 'Or you can go back to the bedroom.'

'The one in the foyer's fine.' Nora Jane had started moving. She was up the steps from the sunken area. She was out of the room and into the hall. She was to the foyer. The keys are in the ignition, she was thinking. I saw him leave them there. And if they aren't I'll walk. But I am getting out of here.

Then she was out the door and past the cupids and running along the paving stones to the parking lot. The Lincoln was right where Sandy had parked it. She got in and turned the key and the engine came on and she backed out and started driving. Down the steep rocky drive so fast she almost went over the side. She slowed down and turned onto the ocean road. Slow down, she told herself. You could run over someone. They can't do anything to me. They can't send the police after me. Not with all they have going on in there. All I have to do is drive this car. I don't have to hurry and I don't have to worry about a single thing. And I don't have to think about Sandy. Imagine him doing it with that woman. Well, I should talk. I mean, I've been doing it with Freddy. But it isn't the same thing. Well it isn't.

She looked out toward the ocean, the Pacific Ocean lying dark green and wonderful in the evening sun. I'll just think about the whales, she decided. I'll concentrate on whales. Tam says they hear us thinking. She says they hear everything we do. Well, Chinese people are always saying things like that. I guess part of what they say is true. I mean they're real old. They've been around so long.

It was dark when Nora Jane got to Freddy's house. The front door was wide open. He was in the hot tub with the stereo blaring out country music. 'Oh, I'm a good-hearted woman, in love with a good-timing man', Waylon Jennings was filling the house with dumb country ideas.

'I'm drunk as a deer,' Freddy called out when he saw her. 'The one I love won't admit she loves me. Therefore I am becoming an alcoholic. One and one makes two. Cause and effect. Ask Neiman. He'll tell you. He's helping me. He's right over there, passed out on the sofa. In his green suit. Wake him up. Ask him if I'm an alcoholic or not. He'll tell you.' Freddy picked up a bottle of brandy from beside an art deco soap dish and waved it in the air. 'Brandy. King of elixirs. The royal drink of the royal heads of France, and of me. Frederick Slazenger Harwood, lover of the cruel Louisiana voodoo queen. Voodooooed. I've been voodooooed. Vamped and rendered alcoholic.'

'Get out of there before you drown yourself. You shouldn't be in there drunk. I think you've started living in that hot tub.'

'Not getting out until I shrivel. Ask Neiman. Go ahead, wake him up. Ask him. Going to shrivel up to a tree limb. Have myself shipped to the Smithsonian. Man goes back to tree. I can see the headlines.'

'I stole a car. It's in the driveway.'

'Stay me with flagons,' he called out. 'Comfort me with apples, for I am sick with love. Neiman, get up. Nora Jane stole a car. We have to turn her in. Why did you steal a car? I just gave you a car.' He pulled himself up on the edge of the hot tub. 'Why on earth would you steal a car?'

So, first there was the night she spent with Freddy, then there was the night she spent with Sandy, then there was the night she stole the car. Then three weeks went by. Then five weeks went by and Nora Jane Whittington had not started menstruating and she was losing weight and kept falling asleep in the afternoon and the smell of cigarettes or bacon frying was worse than the smell of a chicken-plucking plant. The egg had been hard at work.

A miracle, the sisters at the Academy of the Most Sacred Heart of Jesus would have said. Chemistry, Maurice would say. Energy, Mirium Sallisaw would declare. This particular miraculous energetic piece of chemistry had split into two identical parts and they were attached now to the lining of Nora Jane's womb, side by side, the size of snow peas, sending out for what they needed, water and pizza and sleep, rooms without smoke or bacon grease.

'Well, at least its name will start with an H,' Nora Jane said. She was talking to Tam Suyin, a Chinese mathematician's wife who was her best friend and confidante in the house on Arch Street where she lived. It was a wonderful old Victorian house made of boards two feet wide. Lobelia and iris and Madonna lilies lined the sidewalk leading to the porch. Along the side poppies as red as blood bloomed among daisies and snapdragons. Fourteen people lived in the twelve bedrooms, sharing the kitchen and the living quarters.

Nora Jane had met Tam the night she moved in, in the middle of the night, after an earthquake. Tam and her husband Li had taught Nora Jane many things she would never have heard of in Louisiana. In return Nora Jane was helping them with their English grammar. Now, wherever they went in the world, the Suyins' English would be coloured by Nora Jane's soft southern idioms.

'And it probably will have brown eyes,' she continued. 'I mean, Sandy has blue eyes, or, I guess you could call them grey. But Freddy and I have brown eyes. That's two out of three. Oh, Tam, what am I going to do? Would you just tell me that?' Nora Jane had just come back from the doctor. She walked across the room and lay down on the bed, her face between her hands.

'Start at the beginning. Tell story all over. Leave out romance. We see if we figure something out. Tell story again.'

'OK. I know I started menstruating about ten days before I took the IUD out. I had to wait until I stopped bleeding. I used to bleed like a stuck pig when I had that thing. That's why I took it out. So then I made love to Freddy that night. Then Sandy called me, or, no, I called him because I heard this Bob Dylan song. Anyway, I was glad to see him until I met these people he's been living with. This woman that gives drugs to her own kid. But first I made love to him and we cried a lot. I mean, it was really good making love to him. So I think it must be Sandy's. Don't you? What do you think?'

Tam came across the room and sat down on the bed and began to rub Nora Jane's back, moving her fingers down the vertebrae. 'We can make abortion with massage. Very easy. Not hurt body. Not cost anything. No one make you have this baby. You make up your mind. I do it for you.'

'I couldn't do that. I was raised a Catholic. It isn't like being from China. Well, I don't mind having it anyway. I thought about it all the way home from the doctor's. I mean, I don't have any brothers or sisters. My father's dead and my mother's a drunk. So I don't care much anyway. I'll have someone kin to me. If it will be a girl. It'll be all right if it's a girl and I can name her Lydia after my grandmother. She was my favourite person before she died. She had this swing on her porch.' Nora Jane put her face deeper into the sheets, trying to feel sorry for herself. Tam's hands moved to her shoulders, rubbing and stroking, caressing and loving. Nora Jane turned her head to the side. A breeze was blowing in the window. The curtains were billowing like sails. Far out at sea she imagined a whale cub turning over inside its mother. 'It will be all right if it's a girl and I can name it Lydia for my grandmother.'

'Yes,' Tam said. 'Very different from China.'

'Who do you think it belongs to?' Nora Jane said again.

'It belong to you. You quit thinking about it for a while. Think one big grasshopper standing on leaf looking at you with big eyes. Eyes made of jade. You sleep now. When Li come home I make us very special dinner to celebrate baby coming into world. Li work on problem. Figure it out on calculator.'

'If it had blond hair I'd know it was Sandy's. But black hair could be mine or Freddy's. Well, mine's blacker than his. And curlier . . .'

'Go to sleep. Not going to be as simple as colour of hair. Nothing simple in this world, Nora Jane.'

'Well, what am I going to do about all this?' she said sleepily. Tam's fingers were pressing into the nerves at the base of her neck. 'What on earth am I going to do?'

'Not doing anything for now. For now going to sleep. When Li come home tonight he figure it out. Not so hard. We get it figured out.' Tam's fingers moved up into Nora Jane's hair, massaging the old brain on the back of the head. Nora Jane and Lydia and Tammili Whittington settled down and went to sleep.

'Fifty-five per cent chance baby will be girl,' Li said, looking up from his calculations. 'Forty-six per cent chance baby is fathered by Mr Harwood. 'Fifty-four per cent chance baby is fathered by Mr Halter. Which one is smartest gentleman, Nora Jane? Which one you wish it to be?'

'I don't know. They're smart in different ways.'

'Maybe it going to be two babies. Like Double Happiness Bun. One for each father.' Li laughed softly at his joke. Tam lowered her head, ashamed of him. He had been saying many strange things since they came to California.

'You sure it going to be good idea to have this baby?' he said next.

'I guess so,' Nora Jane said. 'I think it is.' She searched their faces trying to see what they wanted to hear but their faces told her nothing. Tam was looking down at her hands. Li was playing with his pocket calculator.

'How you going to take care of this baby and go to your job?' he said.

'That's nothing,' Nora Jane said. 'I've already thought about that. It isn't that complicated. People do it all the time. They have these little schools for them. Day-care centres. I used to work in one the sisters of Mercy had on Magazine Street. I worked there in the summers. We had babies and little kids one and two years old. In the afternoons they would lie down on their cots and we would sit by them and pat their backs while they went to sleep. It was the best job I ever had. The shades would be drawn and the fan on and we'd be sitting by the cots patting them and you could hear their little breaths all over the room. I used to pat this one little boy with red hair. His back would go up and down. I know all about little kids and babies. I can have one if I want to.'

'Yes, you can,' Tam said. 'You strong girl. Do anything you want to do.'

'You going to tell Mr Harwood and Mr Halter about this baby?' Li said.

'I don't know,' she answered. 'I haven't made up my mind about that.'

Then for two weeks Nora Jane kept her secret. She was good at keeping secrets. It came from being an only child. When Freddy called she told him she couldn't see him for a while. She hadn't talked to Sandy since she called and told him where to pick up Mirium's car.

At night she slept alone with her secret. In the morning she dressed and went down to the gallery where she worked and listened to people talk about the paintings. She felt very strange, sleepy and secretive and full of insight. I think my

113

vision is getting better, she told herself, gazing off into the pastel hills. I am getting into destiny, she said to herself at night, feeling the cool sheets against her legs. I am part of time, oceans and hurricanes and earthquakes and the history of man. I am the aurora borealis and the stars. I am as crazy as I can be. I ought to call my mother.

Finally Freddy Harwood had had as much as he could stand. There was no way he was letting a girl he loved refuse to see him. He waited fourteen days, counting them off, trying to get to twenty-one, which he thought was a reasonable number of days to let a misunderstanding cool down. Only, what was the misunderstanding? What had he done but fall in love? He waited and brooded.

On the fourteenth day he started off for work, then changed his mind and went over to this cousin Leah's gallery where he had gotten Nora Jane a job. The gallery was very posh. It didn't even open until eleven in the morning. He got there about ten-thirty and went next door to *Le Chocolat* and bought a chocolate statue of Aphrodite and stood by the plate-glass windows holding the box and watching for Nora Jane's car. Finally he caught a glimpse of it in the far lane on Shattuck Boulevard heading for the parking lot of the Safeway store. He ran out the door and down to the corner and stood by a parking meter on the boulevard.

She got out of the car and came walking over, not walking very fast. She was wearing a long white rayon shirt over black leotards, looking big-eyed and thin. 'You look terrible,' he said, forgetting his pose, hurrying to meet her. 'What have you been doing? Take this, it's a chocolate statue I bought for you. What's going on, N.J.? I want you to talk to me. Goddammit, we are going to talk.'

'I'm going to have a baby,' she said. She stepped up on the

sidewalk. Traffic was going by on the street. Clouds were going by in the sky. 'Oh, my God,' Freddy said.

'And I don't know who the father is. It might be your baby. I don't know if it is or not.' Her eyes were right on his. They were filling up with tears, a movie of tears, a brand-new fresh print of a movie of tears. They poured down her cheeks and on to her hands and the white cardboard box holding the chocolate Aphrodite. Some even fell on her shoes.

'So what,' Freddy said. 'That's not so bad. I mean, at least you don't have cancer. When I saw you get out of the car I thought, leukemia, she's got leukemia.'

'I don't know who the father is,' she repeated. 'There's a forty-six per cent chance it's you.'

'Let's get off this goddamn street,' he said. 'Let's go out to the park.'

'You aren't mad? You aren't going to kill me?'

'I haven't had time to get mad. I've hardly had time to go into shock. Come on, N.J., lets go out to the park and see the Buddha.'

'He has blue eyes, or grey eyes, I guess you'd call them. And you have brown eyes and I have brown eyes. So it isn't going to do any good if it has brown eyes. Li said it's more the time of month anyway because sperm can live several days. So I've been trying and trying to remember . . .'

'Let's don't talk about it any more,' Freddy said. 'Let's talk less and think more.' They were in the De Young Museum in Golden Gate Park. Freddy had called his cousin Leah and told her Nora Jane couldn't come in to work and they had gone out to the park to see a jade Buddha he worshipped. 'This all used to be free,' he said, as he did every time he brought her there. 'The whole park. Even the planetarium. Even the cookies in the tea garden. My father used to bring me here.' They were standing in an arch between marble rooms.

'Let's go look at the Buddha again before we leave,' Nora Jane said. 'I'm getting as bad about that Buddha as you are.' They walked back into the room and up to the glass box that housed the Buddha. They walked slowly around the case looking at the Buddha from all angles. The hands outstretched on the knees, the huge ears, the spine, the ribs, the drape of the stole across the shoulder. Sakyumuni as an Ascetic. It was a piece of jade so luminous, so rounded and perfect and alive that just looking at it was sort of like being a Buddha.

'Wheeewwww,' Nora Jane said. 'How on earth did he make it?'

'Well, to begin with, it took twenty years. I mean, you don't just turn something like that out overnight. He made it for his teacher, but the teacher died before it was finished.'

Nora Jane held her hands out to the light coming from the case, as if to catch some Buddha knowledge. 'I could go see your friend Eli, the geneticist,' she said. 'He could find out for me, couldn't he? I mean he splices genes, it wouldn't be anything to find out what blood type a baby had. How about that? I'll call him up and ask him if there's any way I can find out before it comes.'

'Oh, my God,' Freddy said. 'Don't go getting any ideas about Eli. Don't go dragging my friends into this. Let's just keep this under our hats. Let's don't go spreading this around.'

'I'm not keeping anything I do under my hat,' she said. She stepped back from him and folded her hands at her waist. Same old, same old stuff, she thought. 'You just go on home, Freddy,' she said. 'I'll take BART. I don't want to talk to you any more today. I was doing just fine until you showed up with that chocolate statue. I've never been ashamed of anything I've done in my life and I'm not about to start being ashamed now.' She was backing up, heading for the door. 'So go on. Go on and leave me alone. I mean it. I really mean it.'

'How about me?' he called after her retreating back. 'What am I supposed to do? How am I supposed to feel? What if I don't want to be alone? What if I need someone to talk to?' She held her hands up in the air with the palms turned toward the ceiling. Then she walked on off without turning around.

Several days later Nora Jane was at the gallery. It was late in July. Almost a year since she had robbed the bar in New Orleans and flown off to California to be with Sandy. So much had happened in that time. Sometimes she felt like a different person. Other times she felt like the same old Nora Jane. That morning while she was dressing for work she had looked at her body for a long time in the mirror, turning this way and that to see what was happening. Her body was beginning to have a new configuration, strange volumes like a Titian she admired in one of Leah's art books.

It was cool in the gallery, too cool for Nora Jane's sleeveless summer dress. Just right for the three-piece suit on the man standing beside her. They were standing before one of Nora Jane's favourite paintings. The man was making notes on a pad and saying things to the gallery owner that made Nora Jane want to sock him in the face.

'What is the source of light, dear heart? I can't review this show, Leah. This stuff's so old-fashioned. It's so obvious, for God's sake. Absolutely no restraint. I can't believe you got me over here for this. I think you're going all soppy on me.'

'Oh, come on,' Leah said. 'Give it a chance, Ambrose. Put the pad away and just look.'

'I can't look, angel. I have a trained eye.' Nora Jane sighed. Then she moved over to the side of the canvas and held the edge of the frame in her hand. It was a painting of a kimono being lifted from the sea by a dozen seagulls. A white kimono with purple flowers being lifted from a green sea. The gulls were carrying it in their beaks, each gull in a different pose. Below the painting was a card with lines from a book.

On some undressed bodies the burns made patterns . . . and on the skin of some women . . . the shapes of flowers they had had on their kimonos . . .

Hiroshima, by John Hersey

'Hummm . . .' Nora Jane said. 'The source of light? This is a painting, not a light bulb. There's plenty of light. Every one of those doves is a painting all by itself. I bet it took a million hours just to paint those doves. This is a wonderful painting. This is one of the most meaningful paintings I ever saw. Anybody that doesn't know this painting is wonderful isn't fit to judge a beauty contest at a beach, much less a rock of art, I mean, a work of art.'

'Leah,' the man said. 'Who is this child?'.

'I used to work here,' she said. 'But now I'm quitting. I'm going home. I'm going to have a baby and I don't want it floating around inside me listening to people say nasty things about other people's paintings. You can't tell what they hear. They don't know what all they can hear.'

'A baby,' Leah said. She moved back as though she was afraid some of it might spill on her grey silk blouse. 'My cousin Freddy's baby?'

'I don't know,' Nora Jane said. 'It's just a baby. I don't know whose it is.'

I'm doing things too fast, she thought. She was driving aimlessly down University Avenue, headed for a bridge. I'm cutting off my nose to spite my face. I'm burning my bridges behind me. I'll call my mother and tell her where I am. Yeah, and then she'll just get drunker than ever and call me up all the time like she used to at the Mushroom Cloud. Never mind that. I'll get a job at a day-care centre. That's what I'll do. This place is full of rich people. I bet they have great ones out here. I'll go find the best one they have and get a job in it. Then I'll be all set when she comes. Well, at least I can still think straight. Thank God for that. Maybe I'll drive out to Bodega Bay and spend the day by the ocean. I'll get a notebook and write down everything I have to do and make all my plans. Then tomorrow I'll go and apply for jobs at day-care centres. I wonder what they pay. Not much I bet. Who cares? I'll live on whatever they pay me. That's one thing Sandy taught me. You don't have to do what they want you to if you don't have to have their stuff. It was worth living with him just to learn that. I've got everything I need. It's a wonderful day. I loved saying that stuff to that man, that Ambrose whatever his name is. I'll bet he's thinking about it right this minute. *You aren't fit to judge a beauty contest at the beach much less a work of art.* That was good, that was really good. I bet he won't forget me saying that. I bet no one's said anything to him in years except what he wants to hear.

Nora Jane turned on the radio, made a left at a stop-light and drove out onto the Richmond–San Rafael bridge. She had the top down on the convertible. The radio was turned up good and loud. Some lawyers down in Texas were saying the best place to store nuclear waste would be the salt flats in Mexico. Nora Jane was driving along, listening to the lawyers, thinking about the ocean, thinking how nice it would be to sit and watch the waves come in. Thinking about what she'd stop and get to eat. I have to remember to eat, she was thinking. I have to get lots of protein and stuff to make her bones thick.

*

'She was just past the first long curve of the bridge when it happened. The long roller coaster of a bridge swayed like the body of a snake, making a hissing sound that turned into thunder. The sound rolled across the bay. Then the sound stopped. Then a long time went by. The car seemed to be made of water. The bridge of water. Nora Jane's arms of water. Still, she seemed to know what to do. She turned off the ignition. She reached behind her and pulled down the shoulder harness and put it on.

The bridge moved again. Longer, slower, like a long cold dream. The little blue convertible swerved to the side, rubbing up against a station wagon. The bumper grated and slid, grated and slid. Then everything was still. Everything stopped happening. The islands in the bay were still in their places. Angel Island and Morris Island and the Brothers and the Sisters and the sad face of Alcatraz. An oil tank had burst on Morris Island and a shiny black river was pouring down a hill. Nora Jane watched it pour, then turned and looked into the station wagon.

A woman was at the wheel. Four or five small children were jumping up and down on the seats, screaming and crying. 'Do not move from a place of safety,' the radio was saying. 'The aftershocks could begin at any moment. Stay where you are. If you have an emergency call 751–1000. Please do not call to get information. We are keeping you informed. Repeat. Do not move from a place of safety. The worst shock has passed. If you are with injured parties call 751–1000.' I think I'm in a place of safety, Nora Jane thought.

The children were screaming in the station wagon. They were screaming their heads off. I have to go and see if they're hurt, she thought. But what if a shock comes while I'm going from here to there? I'll fall off the bridge. I'll fall into the sea. 'The Golden Gate is standing. The approaches are gone to the

Bay Bridge and the Richmond–San Rafael. There is no danger of either bridge collapsing. Repeat, there is no danger of either bridge collapsing. Please do not move from a place of safety. If you are with injured parties call 751–1000. Do not call to get information. Repeat . . .'

That's too many children for one woman. What if they're hurt? Their arms might be broken. I smashed in her side. I have to go over there and help her. I have to do it. Oh, shit. Hail Mary, full of grace, blessed art thou among women and blessed is the fruit of thy womb, Jesus. Womb, oh, my womb, what about my womb. . . ? Nora Jane was out of the car and making her way around the hood to the station wagon. Holy Mary, Mother of God, pray for us sinners now and at the hour of our death . . . She reached the door handle of the back seat and opened the door and slid in. The children stopped their screaming. Five small faces and one large one turned her way. 'I came to help,' she said. 'Are any of them hurt? Are they injured?'

'Thank God you're here,' the woman said. 'My radio doesn't work. What's happening? What's going on?'

'It's a big one. Almost a seven. The approaches to this bridge are gone. Are the children all right? Are any of them hurt?'

'I don't think so. We're a car pool. For swimming lessons. I think they're all right. Are you all right?' she said, turning to the children. 'I think they're just screaming.' None of them was screaming now but one small boy was whining. 'Ohhhhhhhh . . .' he was saying very low and sad.

'Well now, I'm here,' Nora Jane said. 'They'll come get us in boats. They'll come as soon as they can.'

'I'm a doctor's wife. My husband's Doctor Johnson, the plastic surgeon. I should know what to do but he never told me. I don't know. I just don't know.'

'Well, don't worry about it,' Nora Jane said. She set the little whining boy on her lap and put her arm around a little girl in a yellow bathing suit. 'Listen, we're all right. They'll come and get us. The bridge isn't going to fall. You did all right. You knew to stop the car.'

'I'm scared,' the little girl in the yellow suit said. 'I want to go home. I want to go where my momma is.'

'It's all right,' Nora Jane said. She pulled the child down beside her and kissed her on the face. 'You smell so nice,' she said. 'Your hair smells like a yellow crayon. Have you been colouring today?'

'I was colouring,' the whining boy said. 'I was colouring a Big Bird book. I want to go home too. I want to go home right now. I'm afraid to be here. I don't like it here.'

'He's afraid of everything,' the little girl said. 'He's my brother. He's afraid of the dark and he's afraid of frogs.' 'Ohhhhhhhhhhhhhhhh,' he cried out, louder than ever. 'See,' the girl said. 'If you just say frog he starts crying.'

'Celeste, please don't make him cry,' the plastic surgeon's wife said. 'I'm Madge Johnson,' she went on. 'That's Donald and Celeste, they belong to the Connerts that live next door and that's Lindsey in the back and this is Starr and Alexander up here with me. They're mine. Lindsey, are you all right? See if she's all right, would you?'

Nora Jane looked into the back of the station wagon. Lindsey was curled up with a striped beach towel over her head. She was sucking her thumb. She was so still that for a moment Nora Jane wasn't sure she was breathing. 'Are you all right?' she said, laying her hand on the child's shoulder. 'Lindsey, are you OK?'

The child lifted her head about an inch off the floor and shook it from side to side. 'You can get up here with us,' Nora Jane said. 'You don't have to stay back there all alone.'

'She wants to be there,' Celeste said. 'She's a baby. She sucks her thumb.'

'I want to go home now,' Donald said, starting to whine again. 'I want to go see my momma. I want you to drive the car and take me home.'

'We can't drive it right now,' Madge said. 'We have to wait for the men to come get us. We have to be good and stay still and in a little while they'll come and get us and take us home in boats. Won't that be nice? They'll be here as soon as they can. They'll be here before we know it.'

'I want to go home now,' Donald said. 'I want to go home and I'm hungry. I want something to eat.'

'Shut up, Donald,' Celeste said.

'How old are they?' Nora Jane said.

'They're five, except Lindsey and Alexander, they're four. I wish we could hear your radio. I wish we could hear what's going on.'

'I could reach out the front window and turn it back on, I guess. I hate to walk over there again. Until I'm sure the aftershocks are over. Look, roll down that window and see if you can reach in and turn the radio on. You don't have to turn on the ignition. Thank God the top's down. I almost didn't put it down.'

Madge wiggled through the window and turned on the radio in the convertible. 'In other news, actor David Niven died today at his home in Switzerland. The internationally famous actor succumbed to a long battle with Gehrig's disease. He was seventy-three . . . Now for an update on earthquake damage. The department of geology at the University of California at Berkeley says – oh, just a minute, here's a late report on the bridges. Anyone caught on the Bay Bridge or the Richmond–San Rafael bridge please stay in your cars until help arrives. The Coast Guard is on its way. Repeat, Coast

Guard rescue boats are on their way. The danger is past. Please stay in your cars until help arrives. Do not move from a place of safety. The lighthouse on East Brother has fallen into the sea . . .'

'I want to go home now,' Donald was starting up again. Lindsey rose up in the back and joined him. 'I want my momma,' she was crying. 'I want to go to my house.'

'Come sit up here with us,' Nora Jane said. 'Come sit with Celeste and Donald and me. You better turn that radio off now,' she said to Madge. 'It's just scaring them. It's not going to tell us anything we don't already know.'

'I don't want to come up there,' Lindsey cried, stuffing the towel into her mouth with her thumb, talking through a little hole that was all she had left for breath. She was crying, big tears were running down the front of her suit. Madge climbed out the window again and turned off the radio.

'You're a big baby,' Celeste said to Lindsey. 'You're just crying to get attention.'

'Shut up, Celeste,' Madge said. 'Please don't say things to them.'

'I want to go to my house,' Donald said. 'I want you to drive the car right now.'

'ALL RIGHT,' Nora Jane said. 'NOW ALL OF YOU SHUT UP A MINUTE. I want you all to shut up and quit crying and listen to me. This is an emergency. When you have an emergency everybody has to stick together and act right. We can't go anywhere right now. We have to wait to be rescued. So, if you'll be quiet and act like big people I will sing to you. I happen to be a wonderful singer. OK, you want me to sing? Well, do you?'

'I want you to,' Donald said, and cuddled closer.

'Me too,' Celeste said, and sat up very properly, getting ready to listen.

'I want you to,' Lindsey said, then closed her mouth down over her thumb. Starr and Alexander cuddled up against Madge. Then, for the first time since she had been in California, Nora Jane sang in public. She had been the despair of the sisters at the Academy of the Most Sacred Heart of Jesus because she would never use her voice for the glory of God or stay after school and practice with the choir. All Nora Jane had ever used her voice for was to memorize phonograph albums in case there was a war and all the stereos were blown up.

Now, in honour of the emergency, she took out her miraculous voice and her wonderful memory and began to sing long-playing albums to the children. She sang Walt Disney and *Jesus Christ Superstar* and Janis Joplin and the Rolling Stones and threw in some Broadway musicals for Madge's benefit. She finished up with a wonderful song about a little boy named Christopher Robin going to watch the changing of the guards with his nanny. 'They're changing guards at Buckingham Palace. Christopher Robin went down with Alice.'

The children were entranced. When she stopped, they clapped their hands and yelled for more.

'I've never heard anyone sing like that in my whole life,' Madge said. 'You should be on the stage.'

'I know,' Nora Jane said. 'Everyone always says that.'

'Sing some more,' Donald said. 'Sing about backwards land again.'

'Sing more,' Alexander said. It was the first time he had said a word since Nora Jane got in the car. 'Sing more.'

'In a minute,' she said. 'Let me catch my breath. I'm starving, aren't you? I'll tell you one thing, the minute we get off this bridge I'm going somewhere and get something to eat. I'm going to eat like a pig.'

'So am I,' Celeste said. 'I'm going to eat like a pig, oink, oink.'

'I'm going to eat like a pig,' Donald said. 'Oink, oink.'

'Oink, oink,' said Alexander in a small voice.

'Oink, oink,' said Starr.

'Oink, oink,' said Lindsey through her thumb.

'There's a seagull,' Nora Jane said. 'Look out there. They're lighting on the bridge. That must mean it's all right now. They only sit on safe places.'

'How do they know?' Celeste said. 'How do they know which place is safe?'

'The whales tell them,' Nora Jane said. 'They ask the whales.'

'How do the whales know?' Celeste insisted. 'Who tells the whales? Whales can't talk to seagulls.' Celeste was really a very questionable little girl to have around if you were pregnant. But Nora Jane was saved explaining whales because a man in a yellow slicker appeared on the edge of the bridge, climbing a ladder. He threw a leg over the railing and started toward the car. Another man was right behind him. 'Here they come,' Alexander said. 'They're coming. Oink, oink, oink.'

'Here they come,' Celeste screamed at the top of her lungs. She climbed up on Nora Jane's stomach and stuck her head out the window, yelling to the Coast Guard. 'Here we are. Oink, oink. Here we are.'

What is that? Tammili Whittington wondered. She was the responsible one of the pair. Shark butting Momma's stomach? Typhoon at sea? Tree on fire? Running from tiger? Someone standing on us? Hummmmmmmmmm, she decided and turned a fin into a hand, four fingers and a thumb.

Here they come, Nora Jane was thinking, moving Celeste's

feet to the side. Here come the rescuers. Hooray for every-thing. Hooray for my fellow men.

'Oh, my God,' Madge said, starting to cry. 'Here they are. They've come to save us.'

'Oink, oink,' Celeste was screaming out the window. 'Oink, oink, we're over here. Come and save us. And hurry up because we're hungry.'

MISS CRYSTAL'S MAID NAME TRACELEEN, SHE'S TALKING, SHE'S TELLING EVERYTHING SHE KNOWS

The worst thing that ever happened to Miss Crystal happened at a wedding. It was her brother-in-law's wedding. He was marrying this girl, her daddy was said to be the richest man in Memphis. The Weisses were real excited about it. As much money as they got I guess they figure they can always use some more. So the whole family was going up to Memphis to the wedding, all dressed up and ready to show off what nice people they were. Then Miss Crystal got to get in all that trouble and have it end with the accident.

What they want to call the accident. I was along to nurse the baby, Crystal Anne, age three. I was right there for everything that happened. So don't tell me she fall down the stairs. Miss Crystal hasn't ever fall down in her life, drunk or sober, or have the smallest kind of an accident.

No, she didn't fall down any stairs. She's sleeping now. I got time to talk. Doctor Wilkins be by in a while. Maybe he'll have better news today. Maybe we can take her home by Monday. If I ever get her out of here I'll get her off those pills they give her. Get her thinking straight.

How it started was. We were going off to Memphis to this wedding, Miss Crystal and Mr Manny and her brother-in-law, Joey, that was the groom, and Mr Lenny, that runs the store, and Mr and Mrs Weiss, senior, the old folks, and me and Crystal Anne and some of Joey's friends. We took up half the plane. Everybody started drinking Bloody Marys the minute the plane left New Orleans. They even made me have one. 'Drink up, Traceleen,' Mr Weiss said. 'Joey's marrying the richest girl in Memphis.'

Miss Crystal started flirting with Owen as soon as the plane left the ground. This big Spanish-looking boy that was Joey's room-mate up at Harvard. She'd already seen him up at Joey's gradution in the spring, set her eye on him up there. Well, first thing she does is fix it so she can sit by him on the plane. Me sitting across from them with the baby. Mr Manny up front, talking business with his daddy.

Owen's telling Miss Crystal all about how he goes scuba diving down in Mexico. Her hanging on to every word. 'I'm going to start a dive school down there as soon as I get the cash,' he said. 'I'm quitting all that other stuff. It's no good to work your ass off all your life. No, I want a life in the water.' He poured himself another Bloody Mary. Miss Crystal had her hand on his leg by then, like she was this nice older lady that was a friend of his. He pretend like he don't notice it was there. Baby climbing all over me, messing up my uniform.

'To hell with graduate school at my age,' Owen was saying. 'I'm too big for the desks. I'm going back to Guadalajara the minute this wedding's over. Get me a wicker swing and sit down to enjoy life. You come down and see me. You and Manny fly on down. I'll teach you to dive. You just say the word.' Miss Crystal was lapping it up. I could see her fitting herself into his plans. It had been a bad spring around our place. It was time for something to happen.

'Go to sleep now,' I'm saying to Crystal Anne. 'Get you a little sleep. Lots of excitement coming up. You cuddle up by Traceleen.'

The minute the plane landed there was this bus to take us to the hotel. I'll say one thing for people in Memphis. They know how to throw a wedding. The bus took us right to the Peabody

Hotel. They had two floors reserved. Hospitality rooms set up on each floor, stayed open twenty-four hours. You could get anything you wanted from sunup to sundown. Mixed drinks, Cokes, baby food, Band-Aids, sweet rolls, homemade brownies. I've never seen such a spread.

The young people took over one hospitality room and the old people took up the other. Me and Crystal Anne sort of moving from one to the other, picking up compliments on her hair, getting Cokes, watching TV. I was getting sixty dollars a day for being there. I would have done it free. Every now and then I'd put on Crystal Anne's little suit and take her up to the pool. That's where Miss Crystal was hanging out. With Owen. He was loaded when he got off the plane and he was staying loaded. He was lounging around the pool telling stories about going scuba diving. Finally he sent out for some scuba diving equipment to put on a demonstration. That's the type wedding this was. Any of the guests that wanted anything they just called up and someone brought it to them.

It was getting dark by then. The sun almost down. Someone comes up with the scuba diving equipment and Owen puts it on and starts scuba diving all around the pool. He's trying to get Miss Crystal to go in with him but she won't do it. 'Come on, chicken,' he saying. 'It's not going to hurt your hair. You'll be hooked for life the minute you go down. It's like flying in water.'

'I can't Owee,' she says. That's what she's calling him now. 'I'm in the wedding party. I can't get wet now.' Well, in the end he coaxed her into the pool, everyone hanging around the edge watching and cheering them on. All these bubbles coming up from the bottom where I guess she is. Mr Manny standing with his back to the wall smoking cigarette after cigarette and not saying anything. Miss Crystal and Owen stayed underwater a long time. Crystal Anne, she's screaming, 'Momma, Momma, Momma,' because she can't see her in the water so I take her to the lobby to see the ducks to calm her down.

The ducks in the lobby of the Peabody Hotel are famous all over the world. There's even a book about them you can buy. What they do is they keep about thirty or forty ducks up on the roof and they bring them down four or five at a time and let them swim around this pool in the lobby. I was talking to this man who takes care of them and brings them up and down in the morning and the afternoon. We were on the elevator with him. He told Crystal Anne she shouldn't chase them or put her hands on them like some bad children did. 'You have to stay back and just look at them,' he said. 'Just be satisfied to watch them swim around.' So we go with him to take the old ducks out and put the new ducks in and that satisfies her and she forgets all about her momma up in the pool drowning herself to show off for Owen.

I kept seeing Mr Manny standing against that wall with a drink in his hand. Not letting anything show. None of the Weisses let anything show. They like to act like nothing's going on. They been that way for ever. My auntee worked for the old folks. She says they were the same way then.

Then it's dark and everyone go to their rooms to get ready for the rehearsal dinner. Miss Crystal's in the bathroom trying to do something with her hair. She can't get it to suit herself. She's wearing this black lace dress with no back in it and no brassiere. And some little three-inch platform shoes with that blond hair curling all over her head like it do when she can't get it to behave. Like I said, it'd been a long spring. All that bad time with Mr Alan breaking her heart. Now Owen.

So she finishes dressing and then she orders a martini from room service. She's in such a good mood. I haven't seen her like that in a long time. We're in two rooms hooked together with a living room. I had on my black gabardine uniform with a white lace apron and Crystal Anne's in white with lace hairbows. We should have had our picture taken.

'Don't start in on Martinis now,' Mr Manny said. 'Let's just remember this is Joey's wedding and try to act right.' I feel sorry for him sometimes. He's always having to police everything. Come from being a lawyer, I guess. Always down at the law courts and the jail and the coroner's office and all.

'I'm acting right,' she says. 'I'm acting just fine.'

'Don't start it, Crystal.' I move in the other room at that.

'I'm not starting a thing,' she said. 'You started this conversation. And you really shouldn't smoke so much, Manny. The human lungs will only take so much abuse.'

Owen was waiting for us at the door of the dining room. He was really loaded now, laughing and joking at everything that happened. He was wearing his wrinkled-looking white tuxedo, big old shoulders like a football player about to bust out of it. He had half the young people at the wedding following him everywhere he'd go. Like he was a comet or something. That's the kind of man Miss Crystal goes for. I don't know why she ever married Mr Manny to begin with. They not each other's type. It's a mismatch. Anybody could see that.

Well, this night was bound for disaster. It didn't take a fortune-teller to see that. I found Crystal Anne some crackers to chew on and in a little while everyone found their places and sat down. A roomful of people. I guess half of Memphis must have been there. They were all eating and making speeches about how happy Joey and his bride was going to be. She was a wispy little thing. But it was true about the money. Her daddy owns the Trumble Oil Company that makes mayonnaise. All her old boyfriends read poems they wrote about being married and Joey's friends all got up and talked about what a great guy he was. All except Owen, he got up and recited this poem about getting drunk coming home from a fair and not being able to find his necktie the next day. It got a lot of applause and Miss Crystal was beaming with pride. I'm sitting by Crystal Anne feeding her. The bride had insisted Crystal Anne must come to everything.

Then the band came and the dancing started. Mr Manny, he's sitting way down the table talking to the bride's father about business, just like he's an old man, making jokes about how much the wedding must have cost. I felt sorry for him again. His jokes couldn't take a patch on that poem Owen recited.

Everybody ended up in the hospitality room about one o'clock in the morning. All except Miss Crystal and Owen. They're in his hotel room talking about scuba diving and listening to the radio. They've got this late night station on playing Dixieland and I'm in there to put a better look on it. Crystal Anne's asleep beside me. Still in her dress. 'Night diving's the best,' Owen is telling us. 'That's where you separate the men from the boys.' He's lying on the bed with his hands behind his head. Miss Crystal's sprawled all over a chair with her legs hooked over the side.

So Mr Manny comes in. He's tired of pretending he isn't mad. 'Get up, Crystal,' he says. 'Come on, you're going to our room.'

'I'm talking to Owen,' she says. 'He's going to take us diving in Belize.'

'Crystal, you're coming to our room.'

'No, I'm not. I'm staying here. Go get me a drink if you haven't got anything to do.' She look at him like he's some kind of a servant. So he moves into the room and takes hold of her legs and starts dragging her. Owen, he stands up and says, stop dragging her like that, but Mr Manny, he keeps on doing it. Miss Crystal, she's too surprised to do a thing. All I'm thinking about is the dress. Brussels lace. He's going to ruin the dress.

Then Mr Manny he drag her all the way out into the hall and to the top of the stairs and they start yelling at each other. You're coming with me, he's saying, and she's saying, oh, no, I am not because I can not stand you. Then I heard this scream and I come running out into the hall and Miss Crystal is tumbling down those stairs. I heard her head hit on every one. Mr Manny, he's just standing there watching her. You should have seen the expression on his face.

They don't put lawyers in jail for nothing they do. Otherwise, why isn't Mr Manny in jail for that night? It's been two months since I ran down those stairs after Miss Crystal and hold her head in my lap while I waited for the ambulance to come. I've still got my apron, stained with her blood. And she's still in this hospital, crazy as a bat and they're feeding her pills all day and she don't recognize me sometimes when I go to visit. Other times she does and seem all right but you can't make any sense talking to her. All she want to do when she's awake is talk about how her head is hurting or wait for some more pills or make long-distance calls to her brother, Phelan, begging him to forgive her for turning his antelopes loose and come and bring her a gun to shoot herself with. And Mr Manny. He's got her where he wants her now, hasn't he? Any day when he gets off work he can just drive down to Touro and there she is, right where he left her, laying in bed, waiting for him to get there. And my auntee Mae, that worked for the old people, the Weisses that are dead now. She says that's just how it started with LaureLee Weiss that ended up in Mande-ville for ever because she wouldn't be a proper wife to old Stanley Weiss. They ended up putting electricity in her head to calm her down. My auntee has been around these people a long time. She knows the past of them.

And there she is, Miss Crystal, that has been as good to me as my own sister. Lying on that bed. I'll get her out of there. Someday. Somehow. Meantime, she say, *Traceleen, write it down. You got to write it down. I can't see to read and write. So you got to do it for me.*

How to write it down? Number 1. Start at the beginning. That's what Mark advise me to do. So here goes. I remember when Miss Crystal first came to New Orleans as a bride. It was her second time around. There was this call from Mrs Weiss, senior, and she say, Traceleen, Mr Manny has taken himself a bride and I would like you to go around and see if you can be the maid. She has a boy she's bringing with her. She's going to need some help.

It's a day in November and I dress up in my best beige walking dress and go on around to Story Street which is where they have their new house. She's waiting on the porch and takes me inside and we sit down in the living room and have a talk and she tells me all about her love affair with Mr Manny and how her son has been against the marriage but she decided to go on and do it because where they was living in Mississippi he was going to school with a boy that had a Ku Klux Klan suit hanging in his closet and they had meetings in the yard of the school and no one even told them not to. Rankin County, Mississippi.

Then I tell her all about myself and where I am from and she says are you sure you want to go on being a maid, you seem too smart for this work and I says yes, that's all I know how to do. She says, well, I can be the maid for a while but I'll have to get some education part time and let her pay for it because she doesn't believe in people being maids. I've got a lot of machines, she says. You can run the machines. When would you like to start?

I'll start in the morning, I said. I'll be over around nine.

The next day was Saturday but Miss Crystal hadn't even unpacked all the boxes yet and I wanted to help with that so I'd know where things were in the kitchen. I got off the streetcar about a quarter to nine and come walking up Story Street and the first person I run into is King Mallison, junior, Miss Crystal's son by her first marriage. My auntee Mae had already told me what he done at the wedding so I was prepared. Anyway, there he was, looking like a boy in a magazine, he's so beautiful, look just like an angel. He's out on the sidewalk taking his bicycle apart. He's got it laid out all over the front yard. It's this new bicycle Mr Manny gave him for a present for coming to live in New Orleans.

'I'm Traceleen,' I said. 'I'm going to be the maid.'

'I'm King,' he said. 'I'm going to be the stepchild.'

So that is how that is and a week later the bicycle is still all over the front yard and there's about ten more taken apart in the garage and King says he's started a bicycle repair shop but it turns out it's a bicycle stealing ring and Mr Manny's going crazy, he thinks he's got a criminal on his hands and Miss Crystal's second marriage is on the rocks. One catch. By then she is pregnant with Crystal Anne.

Number 2. This is a long time later. There has been so much going on around here I haven't had time to write any of it down. First of all Miss Crystal got home from the hospital. I had her room all fixed up with her Belgian sheets and pillowcases and flowers on the dresser and the television at the foot of the bed so we can watch the stories. She didn't even notice. She was so doped up. What she had from the fall was a brain concussion. So why did they give her all those pills? I looked it up in Mr Manny's *Harvard Medical Dictionary* and it said don't give pills to people that injure their heads.

Then many days went by. Sometimes she would seem as normal as can be. Other days she's having headaches and swallowing all the pills she can get her hands on. Anytime she wants any more she just call up and yell at a doctor and in a little while here comes the drugstore truck delivering more pills, Valium and stuff like that. Then she'd sleep a little while, then get up and start talking crazy and do so many things I can't write them all down. Walk to the drugstore in her nightgown. Call up the President of the United States. Call up her brother, Phelan, and beg him to come shoot her in the head. Mr Manny he can't do anything with her because she is blaming him for her fall and telling him he tried to kill her so he has got to let her do anything she likes no matter what it costs. But I can tell he don't like her taking all those pills any more than I do.

Meantime King came home from his vacation and start in school. Mr Manny's having to help him all the time with his homework. Much as they hate each other they have to sit in there and try to catch King up. All this time he still hasn't caught up from the school he went to in Mississippi.

Then Miss Crystal she start talking on the phone every day to this man that is a behaviourist. He's hooked up with this stuff they got going on at Tulane where they are doing experiments on the brain. They got a way they can hook the brain up with wires and teach you how to make things quit hurting you.

Well, behind all our backs Miss Crystal she sign up to go down to the Tulane Hospital and take a course in getting her brain wired to stop pain. Then one afternoon after I'm gone home she get Mrs Weiss, senior, to come and get Crystal Anne and she goes in a taxi cab and checks herself into this experiment place on Tulane Avenue and first thing I know about it is Mr Manny calling me to find out where she's at. Then he calls back and says he's coming to get me and we're going to this hospital to see what she's up to. King overhears it and he insists on going along.

Here's what it's like at that place. A Loony Bin. All these sad-looking people going around in pyjamas with their heads shaved, looking grey in the face. Everybody just crazy as they can be. This doctor that was in charge of things looked crazier than anybody and they had Miss Crystal in a room with a girl that had tried to kill herself. That's where we found her, sitting on a bed trying to talk this girl out of killing herself again. 'Oh, hello,' she said when we came in. 'Tomorrow they're going to teach me to stop the headaches. I'm going to do it by willpower. Isn't that nice, isn't it going to be wonderful?'

'Pack up that bag,' Mr Manny said. 'You're not staying here another minute, Crystal. This is the end. You don't know what these people might do to you. Come on, pick up that robe and put it on. We're leaving. We're going away from here.'

'Come on, Momma,' King said. For once he and Mr Manny had a common cause. 'You can't stay here. The people here are crazy.'

'I don't care,' she said. She laid back on the bed. 'I don't care what happens. I have to stop these headaches. Whatever I have to do.'

'Please come home with us,' I put in. 'You don't know what might happen.'

'Momma,' King said. He was leaning over her with his hands on her arms. 'Please come home with me. I need you. I need you to come home.' That did it. He never has to ask her twice for anything. She love him better than anything there is, even Crystal Anne.

'My head hurts so much,' she says. 'It's driving me crazy.'

'I know,' he said. 'When you get home I'll rub it for you.' So then she gets up and goes over to the suicide girl's part of the room and explains why she's leaving and we close up her bag and the four of us go walking down the hall to the front desk. This is one floor of a big tall building that's the Tulane Medical Centre. It's all surrounded by heavy glass walls, this part of the place. About the time we get to the desk a guard is locking all the doors for the night. Big cigar-smelling man with hips that wave around like ocean waves. Dark brown pants with a big bunch of keys hanging off the back. Light brown shirt.

'Come on,' he says. 'Visitors' hours are over. You've got to be leaving now.'

'We're taking my wife home,' Mr Manny says. 'She's checking out.'

'She can't leave without authorization from the physician,' the boy at the desk says.

Miss Crystal's just standing there, this little bracelet on her wrist like a newborn baby. Only she's Miss Crystal. Now she's getting mad. It had not occurred to her she couldn't leave.

'She's scheduled for surgery in the morning,' the deskman says. 'You'll have to have Doctor Layman here before I can release her.'

'Release her!' Mr Manny runs a whole law firm. He's not accustomed to anyone telling him what he can do. 'She's not a mental patient. She can leave any time she damn well pleases.' I look over at King. He's got this look on his face that anybody that knows him would recognize. Look out when you see him look that way. He's very quiet and his face is real still. The guard has come over to us now to see what the trouble is. We're standing in a circle, with the crazy patients in their pyjamas on chairs in front of a television, half watching it and half watching us. Then King he walks around behind the guard and takes his keys. So light I couldn't believe what I was watching. Then he moves closer and reach down and take his gun and back up over beside the television set. 'Take her on out of here, Manny,' he says. 'You can pick me up on Tulane in a minute. Go on, Traceleen, go with them.' Mr Manny, he opens the door and Miss Crystal and Mr Manny and I are out in the hall. King, he's standing there like in a movie holding that big old heavy-looking pistol.

Then we're out in the hall and down the elevator and running across Tulane Avenue to the parking lot. And we get into the car and circle the block and here comes King. He's locked the guard in the Loony Bin and thrown the keys away but he's still got the gun in his pocket. After all, he was born and raised in Mississippi. Then he's in the car and we are driving down Tulane Avenue. I will never forget that ride. Miss Crystal's crying her heart out on Mr Manny's shirt and Mr Manny and King are so proud of themselves they have forgotten they are enemies. That isn't the end.

When we got home I put Miss Crystal to bed and Mr Manny he starts going all over the house like he's a madman and throws out every pill he can find and then he comes and stands at the foot of Miss Crystal's bed and he says, 'Crystal, get well. Starting right this minute you are not going to take another pill of any kind or call one more goddamn doctor for another thing as long as you live. I have had it. I have had all I can take. *Do you understand me. Do you understand what I mean?*'

'He's right, Momma,' King says, coming and standing beside him. 'We've had all we can take for now.'

THE EXPANSION OF THE UNIVERSE

It was Saturday afternoon in Harrisburg, Illinois. Rhoda was lying on the bed with catalogues all around her, pretending to be ordering things. It was fall outside the window, Rhoda's favourite time of year. 'The fall is so poignant,' she was fond of saying. This fall was more poignant than ever because Rhoda had started menstruating on the thirteenth of September. Thirteen, her lucky number. Rhoda had been dying to start menstruating. Everyone she knew had started. Shirley Hancock and Dixie Lee Carouthers and Naomi and everyone who was anyone in the ninth grade had started. It was beginning to look like Rhoda would be the last person in Southern Illinois to menstruate. Now, finally, right in the middle of a Friday night double feature at the picture show, she had started. She had stuffed some toilet paper into her pants and hurried back down the aisle and pulled Letitia and Naomi back to the restroom with her. They huddled together, very excited. Rhoda's arms were on her friends' shoulders. 'I started,' she said. 'It's on my pants. Oh, God, I thought I never would.'

'You've got to have a belt,' Letitia said. 'I'm going home and get you a belt. You stay right here.'

'She doesn't need a belt,' Naomi said. 'All she needs is to pin one to her pants. Where's a quarter?' Someone produced a quarter and they stuck it in the machine and the Kotex came sliding out and Rhoda pinned it inside her pants and they went back into the theatre to tell everyone else. *A Date with*

Judy, starring Elizabeth Taylor, was playing. Rhoda snuggled down in her accustomed seat, six rows from the front on the left-hand aisle. It was too good to be true. It was wonderful.

It was almost a week later when her mother discovered what had happened. Rhoda tossed the information over her shoulder on her way out the door. 'I fell off the roof last week,' she said. 'Did I tell you that?'

'You did what? What are you talking about?'

'I started menstruating. I got my period. You know, fell off the roof.'

'Oh, my God,' Ariane said. 'What you are talking about, Rhoda? Where were you? What did you do about it? WHY DIDN'T YOU TELL ME?'

'I knew what to do. I was at the picture show. Naomi gave me some Kotex.'

'Rhoda. Don't leave. Wait a minute, you have to talk to me about this. Where are you going?' Rhoda's mother dropped the scarf she was knitting and stood beside the chair.

'I'm going to cheerleader practice. I'm late.'

'Rhoda, you have to have a belt. You have to use the right things. I want to take you to Doctor Usry. You can't just start menstruating.'

'We're going to get some Tampax. Donna Marie and Letitia and I. We're going to learn to wear it.' Then she was gone, as Rhoda was always going, leaving her mother standing in a doorway or the middle of the room with her jaw clenched and her nails digging into her palms and everything she had believed all her life in question.

Now it was October and Rhoda was lying on the bed among the catalogues watching the October sun outside the window and getting bored with Saturday afternoon. She decided to get dressed and go downtown to see if Philip Holloman was sitting on his stool at the drugstore. Philip Holloman was a friend of Bob Rosen's and Rhoda was madly in love with Bob Rosen, who was nineteen years old and off at school in Champaign-Urbana.

Bob Rosen was the smartest person Rhoda had ever known. He played a saxophone and laughed at everything and taught her how to dress and about jazz and took her riding in his car and gave her passionate kisses whenever his girlfriend was mad at him. She was mad at him a lot. Her name was Anne and she worked in a dress shop downtown and she was always frowning. Every time Rhoda had ever seen her she was frowning. Because of this Rhoda was certain that sooner or later Bob Rosen would break up with her and get his pin back. In the meantime she would be standing by, she would be his friend or his protégée or anything he wanted her to be. She would memorize the books and records he told her to buy. She would wear the clothes he told her to wear and write for *The Purple Clarion* and be a cheerleader and march with the band and do everything he directed her to do. *So he would love her*. Love me, love me, love me, she chanted to the dark bushes, alone in the yard at night, sending him messages through the stars. Love me, love me, love me, love me.

Rhoda walked down Rollston Street toward the town, concentrating on making Bob Rosen love her. She walked past the ivy-coloured walls of the Clayton Place, past the new Oldsmobile Stephanie Hinton got to drive to school, past the hospital and the bakery and the filling station. The Sweet Shop stood on its corner with its pink-and-white gingerbread trim. I could stop off and get a lemon phosphate before I go to the drugstore, Rhoda thought. Or one of those things that Dudley likes with ice cream in the lemonade. There was something strange about the Sweet Shop. Something spooky and unhealthy. Rhoda was more comfortable with the drugstore, where the vices were mixed in with Band-Aids and hot water bottles and magazines and aspirins.

Leta Ainsley was in the Sweet Shop. Leaning up against a counter with her big foreign-looking face turned toward the door. She had been in Japan before she came to Harrisburg. She had strange ideas and hair that grew around her lips. She was the Junior Editor of *The Purple Clarion* where Rhoda was making her start as a reporter. She had let Rhoda wear her coat and her horn-rimmed glasses when the photographer came to take a picture of *The Purple Clarion* staff for the yearbook.

'I'm glad you're here,' Leta said, drawing Rhoda over to a table by the window. 'You wouldn't believe what happened to me. I've got to talk to someone.'

'What happened?' Rhoda moved in close, getting a whiff of Leta's Tabu.

'I've been, ahh, in a man's apartment.' Leta paused and looked around. She bent near. The hairs above her lip stood out like bristles. Rhoda couldn't take her eyes off them. Leta was so amazing. She wasn't even *clean*. Rhoda raised her eyes from Leta's lips; Leta's black eyes peered at her through the horn-rims. 'I've been dryfucking,' she said very slowly. 'That's what you call it.'

'Doing what?' Rhoda said. A shiver went over her body. It was the most startling thing she had ever heard. People in Harrisburg, Illinois were too polite to talk about something as terrible and powerful as sex. They said 'doing it' or 'making babies', but, except when men were alone without women, no one said the real words out loud.

'Dryfucking,' Leta said. 'You do it with your clothes on.'

'Oh, my God,' Rhoda said. 'I can't believe it.'

'It feels so wonderful,' Leta said. 'I might go crazy thinking about it. He's going to call me up tomorrow. He's coming to band practice on Tuesday night and see us march. I'll show him to you.'

'Good,' Rhoda said. 'I can't wait to see him.'

'What you do,' Leta went on, taking a cigarette out of its package without lifting her elbows from the table. 'Is get on a bed and do it. You need a bed.' Rhoda leaned down on the table until her head was almost touching Leta's hands. The word was racing around her head. The word was unbelievable. The word would drive her mad.

'I have to go up to the drugstore and look for Philip Holloman,' she said. 'You want to come with me?'

'Not now,' Leta said. 'I have to think.'

'I'll see you tomorrow then,' Rhoda said. 'I'll turn in my gossip column stuff before class. I've almost got it finished. It's really funny. I pretended Carl Davis was Gene Kelly and was dancing in Shirley Hancock's yard.'

'Oh, yeah,' Leta sat back. Unfurled herself into the chair. 'That sounds great.'

'I'll see you then.'

'Sure. I'll see you in the morning.'

Rhoda proceeded on down the street, past the movie theatre and the cleaners and the store where Bob Rosen's unsmiling girlfriend sold clothes to people. Rhoda considered going in and trying on things, but she didn't feel like doing it now. She was too haunted by the conversation with Leta. It was the wildest word there could be in the world. Rhoda wanted to do it. Right that very minute. With anyone. Anyone on the street. Anyone in a store. Anyone at all. She went into the drugstore but no one was there that she knew, just a couple of old men at the counter having Alka-Seltzers. She bought a package of Nabs and walked toward the park eating them, thinking about

Leta and band practice and men that took you to apartments and did that to you. The excitement of the word was wearing off. It was beginning to sound like something only poor people would do. It sounded worse and worse the more it pounded in her head. It sounded bad. It made her want to take a bath.

She went home and went up to her room and took off her clothes and stood in front of the full-length mirror inspecting her vagina. She lifted one foot and put it on the door-knob to get a better look. It was terrible to look at. It was too much to bear. She picked up her clothes and threw them under the bed and went into the bathroom and got into the tub. She ran the hot water all the way up to the drain. She lay back listening to the sucking noises of the drain. Dryfucking. She sank down deeper into the water. She ran her hand across her stomach, found her navel, explored its folds with her fingers, going deeper and deeper, spiralling down. It was where she had been hooked on to her mother. Imagine having a baby hooked on to you. Swimming around inside you. It was the worst thing that could happen. She would never marry. She would never have one swimming in her. Never, never, never as long as she lived. No, she would go to Paradise Island and live with Queen Hippolyta. She would walk among the Amazons in her golden girdle. She would give her glass plane away and never return to civilization.

'Rhoda, what are you doing in there?' It was her real mother, the one in Illinois. She was standing in the doorway wearing a suit she'd been making all week. Dubonnet rayon with shoulder pads and a peplum, the height of style. 'You're going to shrink.'

'No, I'm not. What was it like to have me inside of you? How did it feel?'

'It didn't feel like anything. I've told you that.'

'But it was awful when I came, wasn't it?'

'You came too fast. You tore me up coming out. Like everything else you've ever done.' Ariane drew herself up on her heels. 'You never could wait for anything.'

'I'm not going to do it,' Rhoda said. 'You couldn't pay me to have a baby.'

'Well, maybe no one will want you to. Now get out, Rhoda. Your father's bringing company home. I want you dressed for dinner.'

'How far in does a navel go?'

'I don't know. Now get out, honey. You can't stay in the tub all day.'

Rhoda got out of the tub and wrapped herself in a towel and padded back to her room.

'Hello, Shorty,' Dudley said. He was standing in the doorway of his room with a sultry look on his face. His hands were hooked in the pockets of his pants. He filled the doorframe. 'Where you been all day?'

'None of your business,' she said. 'Get out of my way.'

'I'm not in your way. We're going to move again, did you know that?'

'What are you talking about?'

'He's buying some mines. If he gets them we have to move to Kentucky. I was at the office today. I saw the maps. He's going to make about a million dollars.'

'You don't know what you're talking about.'

'You wait and see.'

'Shut up. He wouldn't make us move in the middle of high school.'

'He might have to.'

'You're crazy,' she said, and went on into her room and shut it out. She had gone to four grade schools. She was never going to move again. She was going to live right here in this room for ever and wait for Bob Rosen to take his pin back and marry her. 'He's crazy,' she said to herself and pulled her new pink wool dress off the hanger and began to dress for dinner. 'He doesn't know what he's talking about.'

Monday was a big day at Harrisburg High School. They were taking achievement tests. Rhoda liked to take tests. She would sharpen three pencils and take the papers they handed her and sit down at a desk and cover the papers with answers that were twice as complicated as the questions and then she would turn the tests in before anyone else and go outside and sit in the sun. Rhoda considered achievement test day to be a sort of school holiday. She went out of the study hall and past the administrative offices and out the main door.

She sat in the sun, feeling the October morning on her legs and arms and face, watching the sunlight move around the concrete volumes of the lions that guarded the entrance to Harrisburg Township High School. The Purple Cougars, Harrisburg called its teams. It should be the marble lions, Rhoda thought. I ought to write an editorial about that. He told me to write editorials whenever I formed an opinion. She imagined it, the lead editorial. Not signed, of course, but her mark would be all over it. Her high imagination. He still got the paper up in Champaign-Urbana, since he had been its greatest editor.

She picked up her books and hurried into the school and up the broad wooden stairs to the *Purple Clarion* office. She sat down at a table and pulled out a tablet and began to write.

I was out in the October sun getting tanned around my anklets when it occurred to me that we have been calling our teams the wrong names. Purple Cougars, what does that mean? There aren't any cougars in Harrisburg. No one even knows what one is. When we try to make a homecoming float no one knows what one looks like. Everyone is always running around with encyclopedias in the middle of the night trying to make a papier-mâché cougar.

We should be the marble lions. Look at what is out in front of the school. Just go and look . . .

'What you doing, Scoop? I was just looking for you.' It was Philip Holloman.

'Oh, God, I've got this great idea for an editorial. Leta said I could write one whenever I got in the mood. You want to hear it?'

'I have a letter for you.' He was wearing his blue windbreaker. He looked just like Bob Rosen. They had matching windbreakers, only Bob's was beige. She had been in the arms of Bob Rosen's beige windbreaker and here was Philip's blue one, not two feet away. He was holding out a letter to her. A small white envelope. She knew what it was. At her house there were three of them wrapped in blue silk in the bottom of her underwear drawer.

'Why did he write me here?'

'I don't know. Look at the address. Isn't that a kick? God, I miss him. I miss him every day.' She took the letter. *To,* Miss Scoop Cheetah, R. K. Manning, Ltd., *The Purple Clarion,* Harrisburg Township High School, Harrisburg, Illinois.

In the left-hand corner it said: Rosen, Box 413, University of Illinois, Champaign-Urbana, Illinois.

Rhoda took the letter and held it in her hand, getting it wet from her palms, and left her notebook on the table with her editorial half-finished and excused herself, breathing, still breathing, barely breathing, and went out into the hall. Philip watched her from the vantage point of eighteen years old. He liked Rhoda Manning. Everyone that knew her liked her.

People that understood her liked her and people that thought she was crazy did too. Rosen was going to direct her career and someday marry her. That was clear. Anybody could see what was going to happen. She was on her way. She was going to set Harrisburg Township High School on its ear. Rosen had decreed it.

Dear Cheetah, [the letter began. Rhoda had found a quiet place in the abandoned lunchroom.]

I am going to be home this coming weekend. November 1, 2, and 3. If you will be waiting for me wearing a black sweater and skirt and brown shoes and get that hair cut into a pageboy I'll be over about 6.30 to take you to the ball game in Benton. If you have to wear your cheerleading things (Is there a freshman-sophomore game that night?) you can bring the black skirt and sweater and change at my cousin Shelton's house.

If you show up in that pink dress looking like Shirley Temple you will have to find someone else to violate the Mann Act with. I have been thinking about you more than seems intelligent.

Things aren't going well up here now. I have had to miss a lot of classes and will have to go to Saint Louis on the 4th for some more surgery. Mother is coming from Chicago. Tell Philip. I left it out of his letter.

Did you read that style book I sent you? You *must* study that or no one will ever take your pieces seriously. Leave the feature section to the idiots. We are after news.

Love,
Bob

She went home that afternoon and took the other letters out of their drawer and got up on her bed and read them very slowly, over and over again.

Dear Cheetah,

I made it to Champaign-Urbana in the midst of the worst winter storm in history. They want me. They took me over and showed me the Journalism Department. You wouldn't believe how many typewriters they have. It must be twenty.

Coleman Hawkins is going to play here next week. Stay away from those Nabs. See you soon. In a hurry.

Love,
Bob

Dear Cheetah,

My roommate brought a cake from home and a cute habit of picking his nose when he studies. The classes look like a snap except for Biology which is going to require 'thought and memory'. This Williard guy teaching it has decided that science will save the world and I am going to sit on the front row and keep him from finding out I'm a History major. If at all possible.

Mother cursed out the Lieutenant Governor of Illinois at a street corner. Where in the hell do you think you're going, she was muttering and I looked at the license plate and it said 2.

Remember what I told you about those tryouts. Team up with Letitia and don't think about anything but the routine. And remember what I told you about talking to Harold about writing the play. You can do it if I did.

Big kisses,
Bob

Dear Cheetah,

I was sick in bed for two days and still can't go to class. I've memorized everything in the room including the nosepicker's daily Bible study guide. Here's his program for the day.

FOR SEPTEMBER 29

DO'S AND DON'TS

Do decide that those in power are there to take care of you. Do listen when they speak for they are there by the will of the Lord for your benefit. Honour the ones the Lord has put over you to help you on the way to your recovery from the sickness and disease of ignorance of the Lord.

Don't be one of those that question the wisdom of older people. Sit at the feet of your parents and teachers. Let love be on our face and shine unto them the light of the Lord.

Don't let vice call out to you. The devil is everywhere. Be on the lookout for his messengers. Do not be fooled by smiles and flattery.

The nosepicker suspects me of being in the legions of the devil. He has asked to be transferred to another room. If the devil *is* on my side that will happen soon. I cough as much as possible and ask him what the Bible is and try to get into as many conversations as possible tidbits about my mother's notoriously filthy mouth. I can't wait till you meet her. She is coming to Harrisburg this summer to stay with grandmother and me.

I'm tired a lot but it's better. Write me. I love your letters and get some good laughs.

What is happening about the play? What did Harold say?

Love,
Bob

Dear Cheetah,
Back in class. Your letter came Monday. That's great

about the play. I think you should call it Harrisburg Folly's, not Follies. Or something better. We'll work on it when I'm home Christmas.

Why skits? How many? Too busy to make this good. Hope you can read it. Out the door.

Bob

That was it. The entire collection. Rhoda folded them neatly back into their creases and put them in their envelopes and wrapped them in the silk scarf and put them beside the bed on the table. Then she rolled the pillow under her head. He's coming home, she said to herself as she cuddled down into the comforter and fell asleep. He is coming home. He's coming over here and get me and take me to Benton to the game. I'm not eating a bite until Friday. I will eat one egg a day until he gets here. I'll be so beautiful. He will love me. He'll do it to me. He doesn't even know I started. I might tell him. Yes, I'll tell him. I can tell him anything. I love him. I love him so much I could die.

Then it was Tuesday, then it was Wednesday, then it was an interminable Thursday and Rhoda was starving by the time she dragged herself home from school and went into the kitchen and boiled her daily egg.

'You are going to eat some supper, young lady,' her mother said. 'This starvation routine is going to stop.'

'I ate at school. Please leave me alone, Mother. I know what I'm doing.'

'You look terrible, Rhoda. Your cheeks are gaunt and you aren't sleeping well. I heard you last night. And I know what it's about.'

'What's it about? What do you know?'

'It's about that Jewish boy, that Rosen boy you're going to

go to Benton with. I don't know about your driving over there with him all alone, Rhoda. Your father's coming home tomorrow night. I don't know what he's going to say.'

'Philip Holloman and Letitia's sister, Emily, are driving over with us. I mean, he's the editor of the paper. That ought to be enough chaperones. Emily's going. You call her mother and see.' If her mother did call, Rhoda would have to try something else. 'Call Emily's mother and see. We're going together. The ex-editor of my newspaper I happen to write for and the editor this year and Letitia's sister. I guess that's enough for anybody. I am so lucky to get to go with them, with some people that have some sense instead of those idiots in my grade.'

'Well, if Emily's going.'

'She's going.'

'Please eat some supper.'

'I can't eat supper. I can barely fit in my cheerleader skirt. Did you finish the black one? I have to have it. Is it done yet?'

'It's on the worktable. We'll try it on after dinner. I don't know why they want you to have black. I think it's very unflattering on young girls.'

'It's just what they want.' Rhoda kissed her mother on the cheek and went back to scrambling the egg. She scrambled it in several pats of butter. At the last minute she added an extra egg. If she didn't eat anything else until tomorrow night it would be all right. Already she could feel her rib cage coming out. She would be so beautiful. So thin. Surely he would love her.

'That's really all you're going to eat?'

'That's all. I ate a huge lunch.' She dumped the scrambled eggs onto a plate and went out of the kitchen and through the living room and sat in the alcove of the stairs, with the phone sitting about three feet away. Soon it would be tomorrow. It would ring and his voice would be on the line and he would call her Cheetah and then he would be there and she would be in his arms and life would begin.

Then death will come, she remembered. Then you will die and be inside a coffin in a grave. Forever and ever and ever, world without end, amen. Rhoda shivered. It was true. Death was true. And she was included. She ate the eggs.

Then it was Friday, then Friday night. Then he was there, standing in her living room, with his wide brow and his wide smile and his terrible self-confidence, not the least bit bothered by her mother's lukewarm welcome or that her father didn't come out of the dining room to say hello. Then they were out the door and into his car and it was just as she had dreamed it would be. The quality of his skin when she touched his arm, the texture, was so pure, so white, even in the dark his skin was so white. He was sick and his body was fighting off the sickness and the sickness was in the texture of his skin but something else was there too. Power, will, something like his music was there, something going forward, driving, something that was not going to let him die. She wanted to ask him about the sickness, about St Louis, about the operations, but she did not dare. The forward thing, the music, would not allow it. Even Rhoda, as much as she always talked of everything, knew not to talk of that. So she was quiet, and kept her hand on his arm as he drove the car. She waited.

'I'm so goddamn proud of you,' he said. 'You're doing it. You're going to do it, just like I said you would.'

'It's just because of you,' she answered. 'It's just to make you like me. Oh, hell, now I'm going to cry. I'm pretty sure I'm going to cry.' He stopped the car on the side of the road and pulled her into his arms and began to kiss her. There was a part of her rib cage in the back that was still sort of fat but not too fat. If I was standing up I'd be skinny, she decided. It's not fair to kiss sitting down.

'You don't ever wait for anything, do you?' he said. 'I had meant to make you wait for this.' He handed it to her. Put it in her hand. The metal cut into her palm, the ruby in the centre embedded in her palm. 'You'll have to wear it on the inside of your bra. We aren't supposed to give them to children.

'I'm not a child. You know I'm not a child.'

'Yeah, well Tau chapter of ZBT doesn't know anything except you're a freshman in high school. Don't get me thinking about it.'

'Are you giving me this pin or not?'

'I'm giving it to you.' He turned her around to face him. 'I'm giving it to you because I'm in love with you.' He laughed out loud, his wonderful laugh, the laugh he had been laughing the first time she laid eyes on him, when he was leaning up against the concrete block wall of the Coca-Cola bottling plant picking her out to be his protégée. 'I'm in love with a girl who is fourteen years old.'

'Say it again,' she said. 'Say you love me.'

'After the ball game.'

'No, right now. In front of Janet Allen's house. Right here, so I'll always remember where it was.'

'I love you. In this Plymouth in front of Janet Allen's house.' Then he kissed her some more. There were a lot of long crazy kisses. Then Rhoda pinned the ZBT pin to the inside of her bra and later, every time she jumped up to cheer at the ball game she could feel it scratch against her skin and send her heart rampaging all over the Benton football field and out across the hills and pastures of Little Egypt and down the state of Illinois to the river.

*

156

On Sunday he went back to school. Drove off down the street smiling and waving and left her standing on the sidewalk, by the nandina bushes. She walked down Bosworth Street to Cynthia's house and sat on the swing all afternoon telling Cynthia every single thing they had said and done all weekend, every word and nuance and embrace, every bite they ate at the drive-in and what kind of gas he bought and how he cursed the gas tank and the story of his mother cursing out the Lieutenant Governor of Illinois. When Cynthia's mother called her to dinner, Rhoda walked back home, trying to hold the day inside so it would never end.

There was a meatloaf for dinner and macaroni and cheese and green peas and carrots and homemade rolls. All her favourite dishes. After dinner her father called them into the living room and told them the news. They were moving away. He had bought them a white Victorian mansion in a town called Franklin, Kentucky, and in a month they would move there so he could be nearer to the mines. 'It's too far to drive,' he said. 'I can't make these drives with all I have to do.'

'We're going to move again?' Rhoda said. 'You are going to do this to me?'

'I'm not doing anything to you, Sister,' he said. 'You're a little silly girl who's still wet behind the ears. I know what's best for all of us and this is what we're going to do. You're going to love it there.'

'I'm going to have a play,' she said. 'I've just written the Senior Play. I have written the Senior Play for the whole school. They're going to put it on. Are you listening to me?' No one else said a word. It was only Rhoda and her father. Her mother was on the green chair with her arms around

Dudley. 'I won't leave. I don't believe you'd do this to me. You can't do this to me.'

He lifted his chin. He stuck his hands in his pockets. Their eyes met. 'You do what I tell you to do, Miss Priss. I'm the boss of this family.'

'He can't do this to me.' Rhoda turned to her mother. 'You can't let him do this. You can't let it happen.'

'I tried, my darling,' her mother said. 'I have told him a hundred times.'

'I won't go,' Rhoda said. 'I'll stay here and live with Cynthia.' Then she was out the door and running down the street and was gone a long time walking the streets of Harrisburg, Illinois, trying to believe there was something she could do.

Four weeks later the yellow moving van pulled up in front of the house on Rollston Street and the boxes and furniture and appliances were loaded on the van. Rhoda stayed down the street at Mike Ready's house talking and listening to the radio. She didn't feel like seeing her friends or telling them goodbye. She didn't tell anyone goodbye, not Dixie Lee or Shirley or Naomi, not even Letitia or Cynthia Jane. She just sat at Mike Ready's shuffling a deck of cards and talking about the basketball team. Around four o'clock she went home and helped her mother close the windows and sweep the debris on the floor into neat piles. 'We can't leave a mess for the next people,' her mother said. 'I can't stand to move into a dirty house.'

'Where's Dudley?' Rhoda asked. 'Where's he gone?'

'He went with your father. They've gone on. You're going to drive with me. We need to finish here, Rhoda, and get on our way. It's going to be dark before too long. I want to drive as far as possible in the light.'

'How long will it take?'

'About three hours. It isn't that far away. We can come back all the time, Rhoda. You can come back to see your play.'

'I don't care about the goddamn play. Don't talk about the play. Let's get going. What else do we have to do?'

Then they were in the car and headed out of town. They drove down the main street, then turned onto Decatur and drove past the store where Anne Layne was working still, selling clothes to people off of racks, a frown on her face, caught forever in a world she could not imagine leaving for good reasons or bad ones, past the drugstore where Philip Holloman would sit every Saturday of his life on the same stool until it closed the year he was thirty-nine and he had to find a new place to hang out in on Saturdays. Past the icehouse and the filling station and the drive-in and past the brick fence of Bob Rosen's grandmother's house, where his grey Plymouth would come to rest. Past the site of the new consolidated school and the park where Rhoda had necked with Bob Rosen when he was still going steady with Anne Layne and past the sign that said City Limits, Harrisburg, Illinois, Population 12,480. Come Back Soon. You're Welcome.

It grew dark swiftly as it was the middle of December. December the fourteenth. At least it's not my lucky number, Rhoda thought, and fell asleep, her hand touching the edge of her mother's soft green wool skirt, the smell of her mother's expensive perfume all around them in the car. The sound of the wheels on the asphalt road. When she woke they were pulling onto the wide steel bridge that separates Illinois from Kentucky. Rhoda sat up in the seat.

It was the Ohio River, dark and vast below her, and the sky was dark and vast above with only a few stars and they were really leaving.

'I don't believe it,' she said. 'I don't believe he'd do this to me.' Then she began to weep. She wept terrible uncontrollable tears all across the bridge, weeping into her hands, and her mother wept with her but she kept her hands on the wheel and her eyes on the road. 'There was nothing I could do about it, darling,' she said. 'I told him over and over but he wouldn't listen. He doesn't care about anything in the world but himself. I don't know what else I could have done. I'm so sorry. I know how you feel. I know what you are going through.'

'No, you don't,' Rhoda said, turning her rage against her mother. 'You don't know. You could have stopped him. You don't know. You lived in the same house every day of your life. Your house is still there. Your mother is still there in that same house. You went to one school. You had the same friends. I don't care about this goddamn Franklin, Kentucky. I hope it burns to the ground. I won't like it. I hate it. I already hate it. Oh, my God. I hate its guts.' Her mother took one hand from the wheel and touched her arm.

'Good will come of it, Rhoda. Good comes of everything.'

'No, it doesn't,' she said. 'It does not. That's a lie. Half the stuff you tell me is a lie. You don't know what you're saying. You don't know a goddamn thing. Stop this goddamn car. I have to go to the bathroom. Stop it, Mother. I mean, stop it right this minute. The minute you get off this bridge.'

Ariane stopped the car and Rhoda strode off across a field and urinated behind a tree. The warm urine poured out upon the ground and steam rose from it and that solaced her in some strange way and she pulled up her pants and walked back across the stubble and got into the car.

'It better be a big house,' she said. 'It had better be the biggest house in that goddamn town.'

MEMPHIS

I

Her horror and fascination with his size. His power, his hands, feet, mouth, dick, all that stuff that carried her across the door of that little frame house on T Street and kept her there until her neck snapped. That's part of it. I have to tell you that part so you'll believe she stayed. I can't believe it and I was there. Katherine Louise Wheeler, Baby Kate, my niece, the daughter of a famous author and a Delta beauty. Cat, Franke called her, and Baby, Baby, all the time when they were doing it. They were always doing it.

'Wait till you meet him,' she said. 'And you will understand.'

'All right. Bring him by.'

'Wait till you see his shoulders. Three people could hide behind his shoulders. His people cleared this land. We owe them their share.'

'When's he coming?' I folded my hands in my lap. I stretched my mind. I am the family intellectual. I am supposed to be able to see beyond my fears. Then he was there. Coal black, powerful, full of laughter. I pictured the children. Light brown with that soft dusty cloudlike hair the children have when black men and blondes breed together. You've seen it. As if a wash of Clorox had been poured across a pickaninny. Pickaninny, what kind of a word is that? Will I never learn? Will it never end?

'How are you?' I said. 'Baby Kate told me all about you.'

'What did she say? What does she know to tell?' He took my hand. It slid into his like a trout returning to water. I decided he was a nice man. I was sure he was the nicest black man she could have found. 'You fix apartments? She said you do it all alone. Make the plans and all.'

'Could I have a drink of water? I've been in the sun all morning. I was playing tennis with some people from the mayor's office.'

I went to get the water. When I returned she was sitting in his lap. 'I have to get on to school,' I said. 'I have to give tests today. I wish I never had to give them. It hurts me more than it hurts them, that's what I always say.'

'It's nice of you to let us use your place, Miss Wheeler. It's really nice of you.'

'Thank you, Aunt Allie,' she said, her eyes as solemn as an owl's. She walked me to the door. 'He has to work tonight. You and I'll cook dinner together. I'll go shopping.' She kissed me. I could smell her perfume. What was I doing in this? I am fifty-four years old. I'm as crazy as a loon.

So first they were doing it in my apartment. The musk from those encounters rose up and invaded the walls. Hours after he was gone I could feel his breath on everything.

I am only a few blocks from the Memphis State campus where I teach. I walked home slowly all that summer. I would stop and inspect trees, read the memorial plaques on benches. Class of 1903. Veterans of World War II, In Memory of Carmen Carson Garth, Class of 1915. Site of the First Earth Science Class, 1923.

It was hot that summer. Hot and dry. The rain stayed over the Ozarks and made us dry. At night the jasmine and catalpa and honeysuckle turned the town into a bordello. The students walked the streets in twos and threes and licked ice

cream cones and hardly seemed to speak and by the twenty-
ninth of June my office desk was littered with pathetic little
notes and scraps of paper. Miss W, can you forgive me? Miss
Wheeler, can I see you after class to explain where I have
been? Professor Wheeler, you won't believe the mess I'm in. I
am so sorry I couldn't come yesterday. If you could wait till
Friday for the paper . . . and so on. Fine, I told them. Sure. Of
course, I understand.

I turned my office radio on to WKSS, Nothing But Love
Songs, and thought about them doing it on my bed.

He came from West Memphis in a rented white Chevrolet and
found her on the university track and told her he was a real
estate developer. She believed him. She had done it with him
a dozen times before she noticed the scars on his neck or
finally got stoned or drunk enough to ask for details. He told
her the truth. I'll say that for him. He never told any of us a lie.
And it was true he knew the mayor.

His name was Franke Brown and his father was a janitor
and his mother collected welfare and Baby Kate thought she
had finally found a way to get her father to notice her, to
acknowledge she was here. Her father, my brother, Hailey
Wheeler. He wrote all those books about man's inhumanity to
man. He sat on Big Hodding's right hand when they inte-
grated the Delta schools. He knew Walker Percy and Shelby
Foote and all the big ones. He had been the hit of a thousand
New York cocktail parties, telling anyone who would listen
about where he stood and what it has cost him in family and
friends and inheritance and now here he was confronted with
Baby Kate doing it with the biggest black man who had ever
stood as a guest in our entrance hall. Well, he lost it, as the
children say. The whole pack of cards came down.

'Get out,' he told her. 'How dare you bring that trash into

my house.' He let her take her clothes. Whatever she could fit into her car.

She came to me. What's an old maid for but to take in the strays? 'He can't live here too,' I told her. 'The place is too small. But you can do it while I'm gone to class.'

Baby Kate Wheeler. Long bones, long undulations, arms swinging free, gold hair like Hailey's, the sweetest voice in the world, a voice like music. Why couldn't her father love her? He loves me, an ugly older sister whose only grace is that I can read his books. Hailey Wheeler, poet, novelist, Memphis, Tennessee's bright troubled darling son.

I read his books and I loved his wife, Baby Kate and Cauley's mother. I loved her every drunken moment she was here, every drunken afternoon and night until she died. I found the body myself, or found it seconds after Celestine. I was the one to wipe the vomit off the pillow before the others came.

The coroner was 'worried' about that, as he told me several times in the mess that followed. 'Not deeply worried,' as he said. 'Troubled. Of course, we all knew Mrs Wheeler drank.'

Anyway, Hailey loved me and I wasn't beautiful in any part so why couldn't he love his daughter, or pretend to love her, or say he loved her or even quit criticizing her long enough to let her love herself? She spent more time getting dressed than anyone I had ever known.

'If only I were prettier,' she was always saying. 'If only my face wasn't so thin. If only I had been a beauty like my mother.'

Hailey was sitting in the police chaplain's car when I drove up. He was in the backseat with his head bowed. This little shabby-looking chaplain was up front turned around to him

on the seat, his hands on the seat belt. I didn't know what to
do. I decided to wait. 'They took the guy away already.' A
black girl perched on top of a Peugeot bicycle was holding
court on the sidewalk facing the murder door. A white frame
house with a porch and a central door framed by windows.
You could see men standing in the yellow light through the
gauze curtains. The sun was going down behind the roof. The
black girl spoke again. 'She's lying in the doorway. They have
to step over her every time they go in. You watch when they
open the door. You can see her feet or something covered with
a sheet. She's right there. It could have been an accident.'

'Aunt Allie, you must believe me I am doing all I can to keep it
at bay.' That's what she told me in the beginning. 'I keep
talking all the time and I barely let him do it to me. I'm not
good at doing it with him. I bet he wishes I was a black girl, a
passionate woman. I'm trying not to love him. I know I'm
trying not to. Something's holding me back.' I turned from the
stove where I was making breakfast. It must have been a
Sunday, right after she moved in with me. Before they got the
place on T. 'Then why are you doing it at all?'
   'I have to,' she said. 'I just have to.'

So I let them use my apartment all those weeks and the blood
is on my hands as surely as it is on his. I could bathe in Clorox
and never take the blood away. The blood and the musk and
her voice talking to me on the phone and me believing every
word she said. Why didn't I go and drag her out of there?
Where was my mind? What took my mind away?
   There were no beatings here. That started after she went to
T Street to be his wife. Oh, yes, she married him. That's how
the Wheelers do things. Went down the day before they
moved in together and said, I do. She was paying for

everything by then, even her own ring. She had that income from the Delta land. Not much, but it must have seemed like a lot to him.

Did I know what was coming? Did Hailey know? Answer: we all know everything. It's just a matter of how much of it we're going to let drift up into our conscious minds at any given moment. At least she didn't die in that mausoleum called Summertree. Where the rest of them finished their drunken lives. Three generations of drunks. That's the real history of this family. I escaped by being ugly. Hailey tried to write his way out. Well, it got us too at last.

Here's the tradition Baby Kate found herself in. Her mother choked to death on absinthe and vomit. She should have stuck to bourbon. She could put bourbon away. Memphis. Nobody loves it, it's a hard town. Are they better off in Boston? I don't know. Same old sun, same old rain, same old longing. All is longing, the Buddha said. I don't believe any of that Eastern stuff, do you?

Baby Kate. When she was small I would dress her up and take her for walks or to the park or to shows the auxiliary put on to raise money. The first telephone number she learned was mine. She would call me when she needed me. Why can't I grieve? How long till I begin to cry? Why did I leave the cemetery before they even lowered the box into the ground? She would have waited for me. She would have stood there until every shovelful was patted down. She was a patient child, a patient girl.

How was it then? Did he come up to her and grab her around the waist with those enormous arms and laugh down into her face and snap her back like a soda cracker? Is that how it was? Did she look up into his face and acquiesce, that way she had of agreeing to things, did she allow her death? The coroner kept walking down the stairs and going up to the uniformed officers and moving his arms up and down, and now the whole thing is lying in the ground that was my baby. How do I go on as if the world is a place of goodness and mercy? How will I prepare?

I'm tired. I'm fifty-four. I'm going to take that post at Belhaven and get an unpublished telephone number. If I go on. Dark, dark, dark. 'Come and get me, Allie,' she would say in her little voice. 'I need you come get me.' Meaning Sally was breaking the dining-room furniture into pieces or melting Hailey's phonograph records in the oven or throwing a television set out of a third-floor window or running naked through the streets, a few of the things she did that I was called in on.

Sally, Sally, Sally, she was so very beautiful. Even at the last, constantly drunk and full of vitriol and screaming insults even at me or anyone she could get to stay on the phone. In repose, the mouth would begin its trembling, that imperceptible tremor, and those violet eyes would pin you down. 'Help me, Allie. Why can't you help me?' She choked to death in that bed that had been the general's.

Now it's Baby Kate's turn and Hailey isn't talking to anyone, not even to me, and Franke Brown's in jail that probably wasn't even a bad man and I wouldn't talk about it either except I have to. I can't get rid of it until it's told. She had this little banjo. She would sit on the steps and sing 'Rabbit in a Gum Tree, Coon in a Holler.' Of course he must have loved her, even if he killed her. She was a princess, a king's child, thrown down upon his bed like a ransom.

I would go to the jail and visit him just to have someone to talk about it to. What did you do to her? I'd say. How did you do it? How could it happen? Say you did not mean to hurt her. No one could want to hurt her. Could they? Could they?

II

Hailey came home from the University of Virginia in the summer of 1953 and asked Sally Peets to marry him and she did. They were both drunk at the wedding and Shine Phillips handcuffed himself to her at the reception and they had to take him along to the Peabody until someone found a sheriff with a key. Harvey Trump had wanted to marry her, as later Harvey Junior wanted to marry Baby Kate. They own this town, the Trumps do. Baby Kate wouldn't let him press his body against her, even at a dance. 'He's a fairy,' she said. 'He smells like a girl.'

She could have had any of them at first, until she went off to Newcomb and got in all that mess. After that it narrowed down and she came home and enrolled at Memphis State and started drinking at night with English department people who idolized her father. She'd get drunk and tell them how cold he was to her and they would eat it up. Knowing Hailey was a bad father made up to them for his books. The books did all right. He was 'legit', as he was fond of saying. Of course that wasn't what he wanted. He wanted to be great.

The black girl was perched precariously on the seat of the Peugeot with her feet on the back wheel. Only the kickstand was holding her up. The good-looking coroner in the beige suit and the built-up heels kept running in and out of the house conferring with the uniformed policeman, telling them what the men inside were figuring out. He was so angry, I loved him for being angry. I could not get mad. I could not register this death. This death was one too many, all I wanted to do all afternoon was laugh.

The coroner kept stepping over the obstruction in the doorway and coming out and going over to the policemen and raising his arms like wings and snapping them back like he was breaking somebody's back. Let it be her neck, I'd think each time he did it. Not her back. Not her precious back.

The crowd around the Peugeot. Mothers and children. The sun going down behind the death house. A long time seemed to be going by. Mosquitoes began to bite. An old friend of Baby Kate's named St John Wells came walking up the sidewalk wearing a white T-shirt. He was coming to borrow some dope. He didn't have the vaguest notion what he was walking into. There were police cars all over the place. He just kept walking up, smiling like an idiot. What was he smiling about? Hailey got out of the chaplain's car and ran out into the street and grabbed St John and started crying in his arms. A mother slapped a child for pointing. 'Don't point,' she said, in a cold tight voice.

'I'm scared,' the child said.

'You have a right to be,' I said. I patted the child on the shoulder and went over and took my brother's hand but he was burrowed into St John's faded T-shirt. 'She's dead,' he kept saying. 'She's dead. A nigger killed her.'

All those weeks they were doing it in my apartment. He was so nice, as nice as he could be. Helpful, bringing flowers and wine. He told me he'd been in some trouble. 'What happened?' I asked Baby Kate later. 'What was he talking about?'

'He fixes apartments. He buys one and fixes it up, then sells it and buys another one. The reason he got in trouble with the law was someone burned one down and tried to blame it on him. Black people have so much trouble when something like that happens. They can't just call a lawyer like we do. So he lost a lot of money. He's just starting over.'

'How does he have so much free time in the daytime?'

'He makes it up at night. Don't you notice he isn't around much at night?'

'Oh,' I said. 'Of course. I understand.'

The faces around the Peugeot. They didn't care. They didn't give a damn. They weren't surprised. What had they heard? What had been going on? What did they know?

'It's going to be on Channel Six at ten,' the man from the panel truck was saying to the rest. 'You can see it then.'

Anybody in my family could tell a version of this. This is the real story. Of whisky and slaves and bored women and death. Two hundred years of slavery and still going on and still paying for it.

Here's the way it was. Here's the first thing I see when I try to understand, try to find a series of events to follow. That house, Summertree at the end of the cold lawns. Sally, drunk in the den, the stereo blaring, Leontyne Price singing Aida. Hailey writing in his den, standing at a stand-up desk, reminiscent of you-know-who. Big glass of bourbon by his side, you-know-who, long half-comprehensible sentences, you-know-who. The servants smoking on the back veranda. Baby Kate on her little wooden rocking horse. Black faces all around her. She is eating a Popsicle, or a bowl of potato chips, anything she wants.

'Come on, honey,' I would say and she would drag the wooden horse across the floor and take it with us.

I am watching my angel die. Through that door. Every time the good-looking clubfooted coroner steps over the door. 'It's

171

right there,' the girl on the Peugeot says. 'It's right in the doorway. They said he beat her with a horse. They took it off when they took him. Some horse toy.'

I walk over to the girl. 'Don't say any more about this,' I say. 'Get out of here. All of you, get out of here. That's my niece over there. That dead child is my angel. My baby, my little girl. Get out of here. Get the hell out of here.' I am yelling now. At all of them, at every one of them. 'Go back inside your houses. Stop watching this. How dare you be here. You goddamn stupid worthless pointless television-watching idiots, get back inside, get out of my sight. I cannot bear the sight of you.'

Three officers had me by the arms. The chaplain spoke, 'Why are you so angry?' the chaplain said. 'Why are you so full of anger?'

'Oh, Allie,' Hailey was right behind them. 'For God's sake, don't make a scene.'

III

The first time Franke beat her up was not in my apartment. It was in July after a cocktail party she dragged him to at the museum.

'It was my fault,' she told me. We were in my car. I was taking her to the dentist to get her teeth fixed. 'I took him there to show him off. To make them look at him. It wasn't fair. It wasn't his fault. I forgive him.'

'No,' I said. 'Forgiveness is for what you can't understand. You are part of this. If you understand, you are part of it. Are you part of it, Baby Kate? Of beating yourself up? Of breaking your teeth? Didn't you have enough of that when your mother was alive?'

'I don't care. It doesn't matter. Those are only words. I love him, which is not words, which is real. Which I will stand by.'

'You must go to her,' I told Hailey. 'He beat her up. He broke two of her teeth.'

'She has made her bed,' he said. 'I'm done with it. Done with her.'

'No, you have to intervene. Someone has to.'

'Leave me alone,' he said. He went upstairs. I heard the door to his office close like a coffin lid. I went out onto the back porch looking for her old horse. 'Where's that wooden horse of Miss Baby Kate's?' I said to Celestine, who was sitting at the table pretending to shell peas. 'Where'd you put her horse?'

'It's upstairs on the third floor with her stuff. He said not to let her have none of it.'

'Well, I'm getting that horse.' I went upstairs and found it on top of some boxes of books and picked it up. It was a wonderful hand-carved creature, a golden palomino with a dark gold mane and a red saddle with a design like coins. Where the paint had chipped away above the eyes the dark grain of the wood showed through. Mahogany or cypress. I patted it on the head. It will bring her to her senses, I decided. It will remind her to ride away.

I picked it up and carried it down the stairs, my mother's stairs, my grandmother's stairs. What is that law? Primogeniture? I'm getting so bad about language. I can't remember the words I need. I carried the horse down the stairs and out to my car. When she was little she would set it up in my front hall and pretend to be out West. 'Dat West', she called it. 'I'm at dat West, Allie, bring me dat sandwich den.' And I would pretend to be the old chuckwagon cook and serve her wild steer and Nebraska grass and buffalo and she would ride 'dem hills'. 'I'm widing dem hills some more,' she would call out and I would say, 'Slow down, slow down.'

'He has confessed,' Channel Six informs me. 'Wife murderer begs to be allowed to go to funeral. Family refuses his request.' Confess, what does that mean? What did he say? What did he say he did to her? Have the gravediggers covered the grave?

I dreamed last night the coffin was sitting beside the grave and all the people left the cemetery and when they were gone the funeral parlour came and took the coffin back to their store and opened it and took her out and returned her to us.

'What a tacky dress,' she said. 'It's torn all the way up the back. Someone get me something else to wear.'

'I will make you a dress of cowslips,' I said. 'A dress of blue flowers.'

The second time he beat her up was on the Mississippi coast, at Hailey's spare house in Biloxi. They had gone down there without permission. The caretaker was rude to them. He called Hailey. He told them they could only stay one night. Then they were treated badly in a seafood restaurant. The waitress wouldn't bring them a menu. Baby Kate was scared. She acted badly. Afterwards he took her to a black oyster bar. She danced with the owner. They walked out on the dunes. Franke hit her in the face. He threw her down in the sand and left her there and took her car and drove home alone.

She came to me. She stayed two days. She got up at twelve o'clock the third night and went back to him. She called a cab and went back to T Street. 'I made him do it,' she said. 'I pretended I didn't know him. I flirted with his friend.'

'You can't go back over there. I won't let you go.' I had thrown myself in front of the door. 'You are not going back over there.' She pushed me out of her way. 'I am his wife. I am going to sleep where he is every night of my life. As long as I live I will wake up at his side. I am married to him. I am his woman. Let me go, Allie.' And she pushed past me wearing a raincoat over her nightgown and went out into the night and I did not see her after that until I saw her dead. Although she called me. 'I'm fine,' she said when she called. 'We're both working. We're doing fine.'

'I'm coming over there and see about you. Tell me the address.'

'Don't come here. Don't any of you come here. I don't want you here.' She paused. 'It would get me in trouble.'

'What do you mean, in trouble? In what kind of trouble? What's going on, Baby Kate? Tell me what's going on.'

'I have to go now, Allie. I have to start dinner. He'll be home in a while.' She was going away. And I could not hold her.

'What are you doing? Tell me what you do.'

'At night we lie on the floor and listen to the crickets and the sound of the people in the neighbourhood and I tell him my stories and he tells me his. We will never run out of stories. We are married, Allie. He is my husband.'

'I have your rocking horse. I got it from your father's. Don't you want it? For a planter. Or in case some children come to visit. You could put it on a porch. Do you have a porch?'

'I don't need it now.'

'Don't you want anything from us? Don't you want to even know we're here?'

'Meet me at the corner of Line and Randolph tomorrow at noon. I'll come and get it from you there.'

'What's going on, Baby Kate? What are you doing? Why can't I come to your house?'

'Will you meet me there? It's a Wal-Mart. I'll be by the main door.'

'Of course I will. At twelve then.' I was there at eleven-thirty. Pacing up and down the sidewalk in my Red Cross shoes. At ten to twelve he came and took the horse from me. 'She had to work,' he said. 'She said to tell you she tried to call. You'd already left.'

'Is she all right, Franke? Are you all right? Do you have everything you need?'

'We're doing good. We're doing fine. I'm teaching her to cook. We're doing fine. Yes, we are.' He drove off in her car. He was wearing a white visor, a white shirt with long sleeves. I don't believe the world I lived to see.

Perhaps I will go and visit him in the jail. What could he tell me? He could say he didn't mean to do it. He could say it was an accident. If it was an accident I might be able to watch the evening news again, to care about my fellow man. Black people. We brought them here. Someone did. Not me. We are being punished for ever, the bringers and the brought. Tautologies, old clichés, pray for us all. Pray for the world.

The crowd has thinned. The girl on the Peugeot rides off down the street. The man climbs back into his van. The whining girl goes in to bed. The chaplain gets out of his car carrying a child's carseat and stows it in the trunk. St John wipes his hands on his T-shirt.

I'm starting to laugh. I've been wanting to laugh for hours.

The white house seems to float above the street. 'Is this a bad neighbourhood?' a woman says. 'I have to know. I just moved here.'

'I don't know,' I tell her. 'I'm sorry. I just don't know.'

TRACELEEN AT DAWN

A lot of people have asked me to tell the story of how Miss Crystal stopped drinking. It seems a number of other ones think it would be a good idea for them too. Miss Crystal is the lady I work for. I take care of the house and nurse Crystal Anne. I have nursed her since she was born and I have been with Miss Crystal ever since she married Mr Manny and moved to New Orleans from Jackson, Mississippi, where her family is. She has a son from her former marriage and that has complicated things.

So we have all been here in the house on Story Street for six years. It seems longer. It seems like so many things could not have happened in so short a time. I have noticed time seems to pass in different ways at different times. Eighteen years since I graduated down at Boutte and that seems like a million years. Two years since Miss Crystal quit drinking and that seems like yesterday.

The reason she had to quit to begin with is that she is able to drink all night if she wants to. Every member of her family is the same way, especially the men. The men of Miss Crystal's family are not like men in New Orleans. They are more like men from a while ago.

Well, to begin with, Miss Crystal's decision not to take a drink was not some sudden decision, like you see on television or like that. No, it was a long time coming. Several incidents led up to it. First, her closest friend told her she thought it was time for her to stop. They were out running on the Tulane track. It was Miss Sister Laughlin that said it. She is Miss Crystal's oldest friend except for Miss Lydia who is out in California living on vegetables. She has become quite thin. Miss Sister stopped Miss Crystal dead on the track and told her she had been drinking too much and it was not good for Crystal Anne to have a mother that was that way. Miss Sister couldn't have said it at a better time. It was only a few weeks after the incident in the French Quarter when Miss Crystal and Mr Deveraux were locked in the bordello trying to stop the child abuse ring. Mr Manny had had to come and get them out and was so mad about it he had moved to Mandeville for good. That story was all over town so I guess Miss Sister had heard it.

Miss Crystal came home from the track very low. She stayed inside all day without combing her hair. Finally she decided she must quit taking a drink if it was the last thing she would ever do. 'How can I do it, Traceleen?' she said. 'I cannot join the A A. They are not my type of people.'

'They might turn out to be nice,' I said. 'Judge Wiggins, that I used to work for, joined them. He is a very nice man.'

'No, I went there once,' she said. 'They are so sad and try to cover it up with jokes and drink this goddamn coffee all the time instead of whisky. No, I will do it cold turkey. I will do it on my own.'

'Call Miss Sister and get her to come over and help you,' I said. 'She's the one that brought it up.' So Miss Sister comes over and they sit in the kitchen drinking coffee and are real serious and Miss Sister calls her brother that is a psychiatrist. We were acquainted with him already. We took Crystal Anne to him once when she was acting crazy and would not wear shoes. I thought he was a very nice man and sensible. He said to let her keep them off until she stumped her toe and so we did.

So Miss Sister calls her brother and the upshot of it is he makes Miss Crystal an appointment and she puts on this light green dress with white flowers on it and goes over to find out how to quit. When she comes back she has this tape. She is supposed to lie down on the den floor with a pillow under her head and listen to it each morning and each night and it will put messages in her brain. Alcohol is your enemy. It is bad for your body and bad for your mind. Alcohol will kill you. Like that.

So Miss Crystal comes home and throws all the whisky in the house down the sink, even Mr Manny's wine that he orders from France, and then she goes in the den and lies down on the floor and listens to her tape.

Then about ten days go by. It is raining a lot and that didn't help. Miss Crystal, she don't let it get her down however and starts cleaning up the house, cleaning out all the closets and the basement and the attic and Crystal Anne's room. I was standing by all I could and even made an excuse to come in on Sunday so as to help her get through the weekend.

Saturday goes by and it is a long day. Miss Crystal, she is used to getting dressed up on Saturday afternoon and having people over. Now what is she supposed to do? The sun was shining. It might have been better if it had not been. By five o'clock she was pacing the floors. 'Go to the park,' I advised her. 'Take Crystal Anne and push her on the swings. I will be here making you a caramel cake. When you get back there will be a cake with icing an inch thick.' That cheered her up. I have never seen Miss Crystal turn down sugar. So she went out to the park and played with her daughter and came home and ate the cake and we made it until Sunday. I let myself in on

Sunday morning about nine o'clock. I'd been up since dawn wondering what I'd find when I got there.

She was sitting in her robe reading a book, happy as she could be not to have a hangover. 'What are you reading?' I said. 'A story about a Kool-Aid wino,' she said. She was laughing. 'This crazy man out in California wrote it. It's about a little boy who is hooked on grape Kool-Aid. It could be me.'

Then Sunday went by and I thought we were out of the woods when who should show up but Mr Manny. He comes by pretending to need some shirts but as soon as he has a stack of them in his arms he turns around and demands to know why Miss Crystal has let Crystal Anne quit school. She is dressed by then, in some plaid wool walking shorts and one of his open-neck casual shirts. He have so few things. It never fails to make him mad when Miss Crystal and King just borrow anything they like of his without even asking. 'Is that my shirt?' he says. Then, 'I can't believe you let Crystal Anne quit school. Children can't just quit school.'

'She is only three years old,' Miss Crystal says. 'Three-year-old children do not need to go to school.'

'She'll never get in Newman if you let her get behind. She has to go somewhere, Crystal. I don't care where it is but she has to start back tomorrow. Tomorrow, do you understand?'

'She said a fat girl was trying to drown her. I don't know if I'll even get her to put her head under in the tub again. She'll probably never learn to swim.'

'You are crazy, Crystal. Do you know that? And my daughter is going back to school. She can't sit in that tent all her life. There's a big world out there and my child is going to be prepared to meet it.' They are facing each other in the hall now. Just like old times. Crystal Anne, she is eating it up, standing in the doorway of the den where she's been watching TV in her tent. I am tired of that tent myself to tell the truth. Can't even get in the den to vacuum.

So Mr Manny has come over and started this ruckus and they fight it out for about fifteen minutes, calling each other Lawyer and Whore and White Liberal Bullshit and Crazy and Mother's Boy and Drunkard and Alcoholic and like that. Then Mr Manny, he go get Crystal Anne and hug her and tell her not to worry he is going to get a court order and take her across the lake where she can live a normal life and go to school. As soon as he is out the door Miss Crystal she walk across the kitchen and call the airport and order a private plane. Then she pour herself a drink. I don't say a word. It is not me she has to answer to. Besides, it does not do the slightest bit of good to tell someone not to drink if they have set their mind to it. Pray is the best thing to do under those circumstances. Hide the car keys and pray.

Anyway, then she pack a bag for herself and Crystal Anne and say she is going to do what she should have done weeks ago, go up to Vail, Colorado and get King. He is working in a ski village up there since he left school. This has not been an easy house to work for. We have shed our tears. I've told you that before.

So Miss Crystal pack her bags and dress Crystal Anne in a new white velvet dress and off they go. No sooner are they out the door than Mr Manny call up and want to talk to her. He seem more reasonable than when he left, talking very sweet and polite.

'Traceleen, go find my wife and tell her I'm on the phone and would she pick up the receiver and talk to me.' Like that, controlled I guess you'd call it.

'They're gone,' I said. She had not told me not to tell. 'She has got a plane to take her to see King. She has had a drink, Mr

Manny. I guess I should tell you that. To tell the truth she has had several.' I felt bad about taking sides like that, nobody in the world could love anybody more than I love Miss Crystal but there comes a time when you must do what's right even if it could be misunderstood. 'Thank you,' Mr Manny said. We hung up and I sat down at the table and put my head in my hands. I was trying to pray but no prayers came. It is too confusing to be alive sometimes, sometimes there are things that make me wish we were all back in Boutte sitting on my auntee's porch without a car. Why couldn't Mr Manny and Miss Crystal just fall in love again and spruce up the bedroom and have Miss Sister over making bread and playing practical jokes on their cousins like they used to do when we were first setting up housekeeping? What has gone wrong around here that no one can love anyone any more?

Then Mr Manny is there and begging me to go with him and we get in his car and go out to the private airport. We got there just as they were taking off. A Queenaire, that's what she hired to take them to Colorado. Mr Manny, he hired us a smaller plane, with just one engine, and the two of us got into it behind the pilot and we are chasing them through the skies. Our pilot has got Miss Crystal's pilot on the radio, trying to make him turn back on the grounds that Miss Crystal is drinking and unfit to charter an airplane. Miss Crystal's pilot, he won't do it, he says only the pilot must be sober. About that time I have remembered how to pray. I do not like the looks of the sky around us, there is lightning going off in all directions. I had never known what lightning looked like before that day. From down below you only see a very small part of what is going on in the clouds. I would have to draw it to describe it to you. I know airplanes with only one motor should not be up in that kind of weather. 'Turn àround,' I said. 'We have got no business flying into lightning.' About that time a big bolt of it went off out the window, a whole network of lightning streaks like a spiderweb or the veins on old people's hands. I thought I would throw up or start to scream. Mr Manny he put his hand on my knee and squeeze it. Then he talks on the radio some more, then he confers with the pilot and we begin to turn around. Miss Crystal's voice is on the radio again and I hear Mr Manny promise her that if she will turn around too and come back home he will go get King himself and anything else she wants him to do, even quit his job. The radio is crackling and crackling. These big lightning clouds are almost touching the wings of the plane. It is the most terrible time I have ever had with the Weisses and even beats the day Miss Crystal threw the television set out the window during the Vietnam war. It is so terrible and the sky is so full of every kind of thing and so many colours I could not describe what they looked like, there is no paint or name for them.

Then I see the Queenaire turning around beside us and we fly back to the New Orleans airport. I thought I must have been gone a year. Mark had a fit when I got home and told him what had happened. He told me never to let him know the details unless I wanted somebody killed.

Part two. Now it is the next morning and Miss Crystal is more determined than ever to quit drinking. It has cost her twelve hundred dollars for that airplane ride. It is getting too expensive to drink and besides, King will be coming home and she will need her wits about her if we are to get him back into a school and off of dope and everything. I wish Miss Crystal had some God she could hold on to in times like these. But no, she prefers to go it alone. So we got Crystal Anne fixed up with Adelaide Simmons to play with and Miss Crystal gets dressed and goes back to the drinking doctor. She is gone half the day. It turned out she was having to have blood tests made.

So this time she come home with these white pills that do something to your blood. If you drink when you have them inside your bloodstream you will become violently ill and think you are going to die. It is called the aversion theory of stopping drinking. Miss Crystal, she thinks it is perfectly suited to her personality as it lets you decide ahead of time whether you are going to drink and not at a party when you are not as likely to hate yourself for doing it.

I wish they could get something like that for the ones that like to eat. Anyway, we have got to wait three days for her to take a pill. You must wait until the slightest trace of alcohol has gone from your blood. So three days go by and meanwhile we are moving furniture. Mr Manny had decided to move back in. They have made a truce. He is only moving into the guest room though. Not into the bedroom. He said they have had so many fights in there, including the time King tore the bedpost off the bed, that he is never sleeping there again. Besides, I think he suspects Miss Crystal has been sleeping there with Mr Alan while he was across the lake. Of course, he is the one that left so he can't throw stones.

So we are moving a king-size bed into the guest room and Mr Manny's big mahogany wardrobe that he takes everywhere he go. He has moved it five times since I have worked for the Weisses, once to Mandeville and once to an apartment on Exposition Boulevard and once down to the Pontalba for the summer. Every time there is a flare-up in this relationship I end up with my back out from moving furniture. I have learned my lesson by now though and have Mark's cousin, Singleton, over to do the heavy work.

So everything is going along fine for several weeks. Miss Crystal, she takes her big white pills and is writing an article for the *Times-Picayune* about how to stop drinking. She had been a reporter when she was young. I think I have told you that. Crystal Anne is in school every morning at St James where they do not have a pool. King is home and has a job working for a man that makes Mardi Gras floats. It is in this warehouse down on Tchoupitoulas and Miss Crystal goes down every day and takes him his lunch. It is beginning to seem like an army camp around our house, everybody on time and doing what they should.

There is this one float King was especially interested in that has the king of the sea surrounded by mermaids and oysters and shrimp and holding a shrimp boat in his hand. He drew it for me on a tablet, then made me come down on my way home from work and take a look in person. He looked smaller than sixteen, in that big old warehouse with them grown men he works with. I do not understand that boy although I love him and could look at him all day, he is so beautiful and golden. Poor Miss Crystal. She has been in for it since the day she had him when she was only eighteen. That's too young to be a mother for someone as high-strung as she is.

Anyway, she is taking her white pills and the children are coming along and Mr Manny, he is just like always. He gets up early and puts on his brown suit and goes downtown to make the money. He is trying to be cheerful but I know he is just waiting for the other shoe to drop. Also, I wish Miss Crystal would break down and go sleep in the guest room. I think it is her place to give in on that and I was on the point of telling her so. Miss Crystal and Mr Manny love each other. If they did not have a strong love they could never have overcome their families and made a mixed marriage. Still, love dies. We must admit that. The problem with Miss Crystal and

Mr Manny is they are too smart for each other and love excitement and love to argue. Sometimes I think it is best if very smart people do not marry each other. There is not enough room in one marriage for so many opinions.

So the winter is going by at our house and it looks like Miss Crystal is going to make her thirty-fifth birthday and maybe even Mardi Gras without a drink. That is her goal. At that time she could tell you to the day how long it had been since she took a drink. She talked about it quite a bit, muttering to herself. Also, she had been finding out about those pills. Antabuse, that is what they are called. It seems that what they do is more complicated than we thought at first. Miss Crystal found this article in a medical magazine that says they might change the middle of your brain where the messages go through from one side to the other and keep the left working with the right. Miss Crystal is very particular about her brain. She was an exceptional student when she was in school and studied philosophy and the Greek language.

Anyway, back to those pills. Miss Crystal had become very worried over this article she read. Also there was an incident at a party she went to. Someone served her a dessert with sherry in it and she became very red in the face and had to leave the table. She was quite frightened by that and had been half afraid to swallow one since. She had been doing so well with not drinking and gotten all the way through Christmas and was enjoying not having any hangovers so she decided to throw the pills away and go back to the tape. Here is how complicated the pills became. We couldn't decide how to throw them away. If we flushed them down the toilet they might get back into the water supply and kill someone down the line. Anything can happen with chemicals. It seems to me that people should be very careful about making anything they cannot get rid of. Finally, we just crushed them up and put them in the attic marked poison, in a sealed can up high where no child could find them. I suppose they are still up there. I should check and see.

Part three. We had come down to the weekend of February 10. Miss Crystal is almost finished with her article for the newspaper and about to turn it in. She was worried about whether they would print it or not as she had not written anything for a long time and she thought she might have lost her touch. I thought it was very good, the part she let me read, but with too many big words. I like writing to stay simple myself, be more like talking so the reader doesn't get the idea they are being preached at. Anyway, Miss Crystal is on a diet on top of quitting drinking and she is nervous and can't sit still. She keep going out to the park and running around the lagoon. Every time she go out there she keeps running into this girl that has this disease that makes her think she is fat even though she is thin as a rail. She is married to this lawyer Miss Crystal knows and she has this six-month-old baby boy she pushes around the park all day while she runs. She is driving everyone that sees her crazy. Miss Crystal wants to get some exercise but every time she goes to the park there is this crazy girl pushing this baby and it makes her ask herself, Am I Crazy Too? Why would someone stop doing everything they like? Maybe I am as crazy as that girl, here I am, almost thirty-five years old and married to a rich man and I cannot even have a drink or a tuna fish sandwich. That is the type thing she would ask herself when she came home from exercising in the park. She had me doing it, wondering what I was giving up, not letting myself do. I am still thinking about that. Who is telling that girl she is fat? Why is she listening to what she hears?

So Miss Crystal is on this diet and she is depressed from being hungry and not being able to decide whether being on a diet is a good idea or something other people have put in her head. She is torn down the middle on that issue. Finally, she comes in the kitchen, it is two o'clock in the afternoon on February 10, I'll remember that day, and she starts making a lemon meringue pie, which is King's favourite. The next thing I know she has me getting out the freezer and Crystal Anne is sitting in the middle of the kitchen floor turning the crank on homemade chocolate ice cream and I am beating up a pound cake. Butter and eggs and sugar and flour and vanilla flavouring and on Miss Crystal's counter there is lemon and evaporated milk and lemon rind and crushed-up graham crackers. I don't know what all. It was spring in that kitchen. I felt like we had gotten somewhere, made some sort of opening. Begun to see the light. That sort of sentiment was in my head.

Life is not that simple. God has made it harder than that. Sometimes I get very mad at Him and think He is not a good judge of things.

Just about the time we are getting the kitchen straightened up and powdered sugar sprinkled on the cake Miss Crystal turns on the radio and this song comes on. A song she used to listen to with Mr Alan last year when they were having their love affair. She stand very still, her meringue knife in her hand. 'Oh, you came here with my best friend, Jim, and here I am, trying to steal you away from him. Oh, if I don't do it, you know somebody else will. If I don't do it, you know somebody else will.'

It is a funny song to have for a love song. I remember Mr Alan standing in this very kitchen dancing and singing along with it, making shrimp Creole and being in love with her. That was when she split up with Mr Manny the first time.

Miss Crystal listened to the whole song without saying a word. Then she reach up in a cabinet and take down a bottle of whisky and pour herself a drink. 'I am going to die when all this is over,' she said. 'And I have not had my share of the stuff I wanted. I am tired of being hungry. To hell with it. I'm starving to death for everything I need.' She drank the glass of whisky and poured herself another one. I did not say a word. I looked at the clock. It was four-thirty. What would the evening bring?

Part four. What happened next I had to piece together from reports. As soon as we cleaned up the kitchen I left. I was not staying around. I put on my things and went on home. 'Stop worrying about that woman,' Mark said to me. 'She can take care of herself.' But how was I to stop? If you are with someone you begin to love them, you hear their joys and sorrows, you share your heart. That is what it means to be a human being. There is no escaping this. Ever since the first day I went to work for her I have loved Miss Crystal as if she was my sister or my child. I have spread out my love around her like a net and I catch whatever I have to catch. That is my decision and the job I have picked out for myself and if Wentriss wants to call me a slave that is because she does not know what she is talking about. Miss Crystal always pays me back. She would go to battle for me. We know these things. We are not as dumb as we seem.

Anyway, back to the night of February 10. I was put out with her that night. She was going to ruin all our good work and there was nothing anyone could do to stop her. The Lord's will be done, I suppose I was saying something like that. That is the will of the Lord. I still think I was right to go on home. Of course, if it had turned out differently I would be feeling like it was my fault. That is also how we are, something we cannot change or do anything about.

The night of February 10. Miss Crystal kept on drinking and cooking and called up a number of her friends and ordered champagne. Mr Manny was in Chicago for the night. Then everyone came over and ate and drank and talked but it did not last too long. Miss Crystal's heart wasn't in it and besides it had been so long since she had a drink she couldn't hold up like she used to. King had come home and grabbed his chance and gone off to play the machines at The Mushroom Cloud. Miss Crystal sent her friends home about nine and fell out on the sofa, just passed right out leaving Crystal Anne alone.

Crystal Anne was being real quiet, taking things in and out of her tent. Dishes of ice cream we found later and half the cake and a champagne bottle. All her dolls and her spacemen and Luke Skywalker and Pilot Barbie. I was the one that cleaned up the tent, what was left of the tent.

It had turned off chilly when the sun went down. None of the ones at the party had turned the heat on and Miss Crystal was asleep so Crystal Anne decided to build herself a campfire. She knew just how to do it. She had watched King do it at the beach. She carried some newspapers out of the kitchen and arranged them on the den rug right in front of her tent. Between the tent and the TV. Then she got some blocks and tinker-toys and put them on. Then she went into the living room and got some of Mr Manny's fat pine kindling he orders from Maine and she arrange it just so. Then she go get all her stuffed dolls and toys and set them up around the edge in a circle and then she took a cigarette lighter she found somewhere and set it on fire. The fire was between where she must have been and the door to the sun room. She was trying to jump from the sofa arm through the door when Miss Crystal woke up and heard her screaming. 'Stay there,' Miss Crystal says she remembers yelling it over and over. 'Go in the bathroom. Go in the bathroom, Crystal Anne. If you don't go in the bathroom I will kill you.' Miss Crystal bust on through the fire and grab her up and run into the bathroom with her and out the back door on to the porch and there is no way down that way but the hanging ladder King got in New York at a fancy toy store. It has been there for years. Miss Crystal didn't know whether to risk it or just throw Crystal Anne off the balcony or try to make it down the hall. From the bedroom door it did not look like the hall was burning yet. She made the best decision that she could. She put Crystal Anne on her back and climbed down with that baby hanging on to her, clawing her face and pulling at her hair but hanging on like a little monkey, as Miss Crystal always described it later. 'Arboreal we were, arboreal we are.' That's how she puts it. It means we used to live in trees if you go along with that theory.

So finally they have made it to the ground on that rope ladder that's been hanging there five years in the sun and rain and then Miss Crystal breaks into a downstairs window to see if King is in his room but he is not there. Then, finally, she calls the fire department and they come and ruin all the upholstery and drapes in the upstairs not to mention the carpets. We were living in the Pontchartrain Hotel for several months after that. It was quite a mess.

That was the end of Miss Crystal's drinking. I wish the story could be of more use to other people. It seems it takes something like a fire or falling down a flight of stairs or getting torn up in a drunk driving accident to separate people from their desire to have a drink with one another.

Of the things Miss Crystal tried the one I would recommend the most is that tape she had. It had some very nice things on it beside the ones dealing with alcohol. Your Body Is Your Temple, that is the one I liked. Whatever you put into it, the next day that is what you will be made out of. What would you rather look like in the end, a bottle of whisky or a stalk of celery or a dish of chocolate ice cream? That's the question I'm asking myself right now. As soon as I finish ironing this shirt I am going to make today's choice. Today it will be one thing. Tomorrow it might be something else.

THE BLUE-EYED BUDDHIST

Sally Lanier Sykes was going to die. There was no getting around that. She was thirty-four years old and she could count on the fingers of one hand the years she had left to sail the British Virgin Islands or dance all night at parties or roll up her hair or paint her toenails or worry about dying.

Sally Sykes only had one kidney and that one used to belong to her daddy and as soon as she got back to Guntersville, Georgia she was going to have to trade it in for a machine. Needless to say, she was having a hard time getting used to the idea . . .

Not that Sally Sykes was going to have to go to a hospital and get hooked up with a lot of boring sick people. Back in Guntersville an architect and a builder and a decorator and four carpenters were working right this minute to build her a room so beautiful no one would ever imagine anything unpleasant could go on in it. In the mean time all she had to do was lie on the deck of the sailboat tanning the backs of her legs and brood about turning loose the sharks in the research station at The Bitter End. The sharks and the manta ray and the puffer fish and the turtles and the angels.

'I am going to do it,' she said to herself. 'By God, I am going to do it.' Among other things it would make a nice addition to her memoirs. Sally was spending the summer writing on her memoirs.

I was born into a world so polite that no one ever told the truth about anything, she wrote, *and into a religion so advanced its members were even spared the discomfort of dying.* Dying, dying, dying. Dead as a doornail. Done. No more rain, no more nothing. No possum, no sop, no taters.

She looked down at what she had written. Several drops of Germaine Monteil dark tanning oil ran down her nose and on to the paper, forming a little lake right in the middle of the page. More drops fell. A little river of oil and perspiration running down the page and on to the mahogany deck of the sailboat. The sailboat was anchored in the middle of paradise. A small cove behind the airport on the island of Tortola in the British Virgin Islands. It was late June, a clear still morning, a paradisal day in paradise. As far as the eye could see, north, east, south, west, up or down, right or left, underwater or above it was paradise. Air the colour of turquoise, water, a million jewelled shades of blue. Air so clean you could drink it, Sally thought. If I drank that air I would be well. There wouldn't be any old filthy blood that needed cleaning. Dirty blood, that's what I'm going to die of. Dirty blood, sounds like a rock song.

Perfumed sweat rolled down upon the memoirs. Sally's heart beat like a drum. Her father's old right kidney strained to live.

I could always ask him for the other one, she thought. He would probably give it to me.

'Sally,' Malcolm called from the cabin. Malcolm was her husband. 'Come down here a minute. Come help me pack.'

She got up from the deck and stretched her arms over her head. She was wearing only the bottom half of a very small emerald bikini and no one looking at her would imagine she had ever been sick a day in her life.

She reached down into the cockpit and stuck an old Bob

Dylan tape into the tape player. *Hey, Mr Tambourine Man, play a song for me*, he was singing. *In your jingle-jangle morning I'll come following you.*

'Sally,' Malcolm said again. 'Please come on down here.' He stuck his head up through the entrance to the gallery. 'Are you sure you'll be all right? Are you sure you don't mind me leaving Jimmy here?'

'Of course I'll be all right,' she said. 'We'll all be fine. Please stop worrying about it.'

'I'm not worrying. I could take him with me.' They had picked up Malcolm's twelve-year-old nephew at camp and brought him along to the islands. He lived next door to them in Guntersville. They took him with them nearly every year. They pretended he was their own.

'It's fine, Malcolm. It's really fine.'

'I don't have to go.'

'Of course you have to go. It's only until Thursday.'

'I don't know.'

'Oh, for God's sake, Malcolm. Please stop all that stuff. Where have Jimmy and Li gone with the dinghy? You'd better find them and get going or you'll miss the plane.'

Malcolm was all the way up the stairs now. He was wearing his crazed look. Except for his height he could have been her twin. Same blue eyes, same golden hair, same perfect nose. He reached out and touched her arm. Oh, shit, she thought, he's going to start crying again.

'You want to make love?' she said. 'We've got time.'

'I couldn't now.'

'We could try. We could lie around on top of each other and see what happens. How about that?' She took a finger and began to draw on his chest, getting suntan oil all over his white shirt.

'Come on, Sally,' he said, 'don't do that to me. This is my

last shirt.' The sound of the dinghy motor interrupted them. 'And put something on. You really shouldn't go around like that in front of him.'

Jimmy came tumbling up onto the boat, holding an old stone gin bottle in his hand. 'Look at this,' he said. 'I found it on the island. Do you think it's valuable? How much do you think it's worth?'

'A lot,' Sally said. 'That might be worth a hundred dollars. Give it here. Let me see it.' She held it up in her hand. 'There's no telling who drank this gin. Some pirate might have had it. Now look here, Jimmy, are you going to take your uncle to the airport or not? It's almost ten o'clock. He's going to miss his plane.'

'Where's his bag?' Jimmy said. 'I'll get his bag. I've got to go back to that island this afternoon, Sally. I've got to see if there're any more.'

'We'll see,' she said. 'We'll talk about it when you get back.'

'Well, I have to go back there,' he said, and disappeared down the stairs. He was a wild scrawny-looking boy with a head of dark red hair.

'That child is so much like his daddy it makes me believe in reincarnation,' Sally said.

'Many people believe in it,' Li Moon said. 'It's an interesting thing to believe.' She had come aboard and was standing beside them with her perfect posture. The two women smiled into each other's eyes. Sally Sykes and Li Moon Cooper adored each other.

'Then I'm coming back as a tree,' Sally said. 'A great big live oak tree. No, not a live oak. A madrone. A madrone tree.'

'You can't do that,' Li said. 'Once you are human you can only come back as another human being.' The women smiled again as if they knew certain things everyone else on earth was too dumb to understand.

Malcolm lit a cigarette and walked to the back of the boat. He hated it when they started that. He hated it when Li Moon sailed with them. He had hated it since the first time she came walking out of The Moorings carrying the tiny little bundle of things she took with her on a charter. He couldn't believe The Moorings had assigned him a woman skipper. Of course, once Sally laid eyes on her she was a permanent fixture. She sailed with them whenever they went to Anegada or down island to the Grenadines or put into the open ocean. In the winter she and Sally kept up an impassioned correspondence, exchanging books and tapes, complimenting each other on how unusual and talented and powerful and brilliant they were.

Jimmy reappeared with the bag. He and Malcolm climbed down off the back of the boat and got into the dinghy. Li handed down a garbage bag full of trash to be taken ashore.

'Don't go to Anegada,' Malcolm said.

'Why would I go to Anegada?' Sally said. 'You're the one that always wants to go to Anegada. Jimmy, don't forget Li's Hershey Bars.'

'I won't forget,' Jimmy said. 'I've got the list.' He started the little seagull motor, letting it idle. Li dropped the dinghy painter into the boat. 'Don't take her to Anegada,' Malcolm said. 'That's an order.'

'Don't forget my candy,' Li said. They all laughed. Jimmy propped his foot nonchalantly on top of the garbage bag, twisted the gas feed on the handle, and the little boat roared off across the flat surface of the water.

'The dinghy captain,' Sally said. 'The one and only James William Sykes. When he was only eleven months old he dragged my hair dryer across the floor and plugged it in and started vacuuming the floor. He was born in his own time. Gasoline and power. All we have to do to keep him happy is keep that little motor full.'

'What do we have to do to keep *you* happy?' Li said. 'What do *you* want to do now?'

'I want to go to The Bitter End and turn them loose.'

'You're kidding.'

'No I'm not. You don't have to help me if you don't want to. All you have to do is take me there. How many are there now?'

'Three or four nurse sharks and some angels. Last month they had a huge angel they caught on the wall. I'm sure it's dead by now.'

'Will you take me?'

'I don't know if we can get there and back by Thursday.'

'Don't worry about Thursday.'

'Who'll pick him up?'

'We'll call and tell him to wait. Will you take me? Well, will you?'

'All right,' Li said. 'Get out the charts. Let's go around the islands. The channel's full of powerboats from Puerto Rico. I'm not going to put up with that all the way to Gorda Sound.'

They went down to the galley, spread the charts out on the table and began to plot the course.

The Bitter End was a tiny resort at the tip end of the British Virgin Islands chain. The University of Mississippi maintained a station there for the purpose of studying sea kelp. They were trying to find a way to cure cancer with sea kelp. Every year half a dozen beautiful tan graduate students came down to spend a year on an island paradise studying sea kelp. One of the things the students thought up to do to alleviate the paradisal boredom was capturing reef fish and exhibiting them in a pen connected to the land by a pier. Visiting yachtsmen could tie their dinghies up to the pier and inspect the fish on their way in to dinner in the evenings.

'The one I really want to get to is the one in Miami,' Sally said. 'The one with the porpoises.' Li put down the triangle. A faraway look came over her face. 'I could tell you things about porpoises,' she said finally, then looked away.

'Like what? Tell me.'

'Not now. It's the wrong time of day.'

'I heard they had one here last year and it died.'

'They kept it three weeks and watched it die. Everyone was very angry.'

Death, Sally was thinking, looking down at the charts. North, East, South, West. Death beating the door down, like a mummy, like a vampire, like dead leaves, like dead fish. Like that. Just like that.

'We'll stay tonight at Foxy's,' Li said, 'then go back out in the morning and get there tomorrow afternoon. You aren't watching.'

'I'm watching. I heard everything you said.' She picked up her coffee cup and rinsed it out in the sink. The noise of the dinghy rose in the air, then came to a stop as it banged into the back of the sailboat. 'What's going on?' Jimmy said, swinging himself down the galley ladder. 'Here's the candy. Wait till I tell you what I saw.'

'Did you tie down the dinghy?' Li said.

'Of course I did,' he said. 'What do you think I am, a turd or something?'

'Come on, Jimmy,' Sally said. 'Don't start that. We want you to act like a grown person. We're going to The Bitter End. We're going to turn the fish loose. We're going to do it, honey. We're really going to do it.'

'Everyone wants to do it,' he said. 'I know a lot of people that want to do it.'

'So do I,' Li said. 'But they don't do it.'

'So we're going to do it,' Sally said. 'You and me and Li are going to do it.'

Out past Salt Island the dolphins found them. Li saw them first. Far out on the horizon, five or six, diving and playing in the water. She watched for a while before she told the others. 'Look out there,' she said. 'Dolphins.'

'That always happens when you're with us,' Sally said. 'You always make that happen.'

'They're good luck,' Li said. 'They bring luck.'

'Should we feed them?' Jimmy said. He was hanging onto the guy wires, leaning out over the safety rail. It was his favourite post when he wasn't at the wheel or standing on the anchor lines. 'They didn't come for food,' Li said. 'They aren't dogs.'

The dolphins were near the boat now, swimming alongside the prow. 'We might hit them,' Jimmy said. 'Be careful.'

'They won't get hit,' Li said. 'You couldn't hit them if you tried.'

'I'd forgotten the patterns on their backs,' Sally said. 'I'd forgotten how strong they are.'

'I could tell you stories about them,' Li said. 'Stories no one would believe.'

'Tell them,' Jimmy said.

'Not now,' she said.

They were far out to the north-northwest of Tortola, headed for Great Camanoe. The boat was sailing itself. Li had trimmed the sails, tied down the wheel and gone below to make a cup of tea. Jimmy was sitting behind the wheel eating cookies and reading *The Pearl*. He had promised to finish his summer reading while he was in the islands. This was the worst one he had read so far. Why are they doing this? he kept wondering. How could they be dumb enough to do a thing like that?

Sally was writing on her memoirs. *Lists of Things Aboard the Wind Chime* was the title of her afternoon's work.

Books *Ragtime, The Naked Ape, The Pleasure Bond, Coming of Age in Samoa, The Greening of America, The Sorcerer of Bolinas Reef, An Unfinished Woman, The Hunting Hypothesis, Fire in the Lake, Trout Fishing in America.*

Drugs. Seconal, Dilaudid, aspirin, iodine, Dramamine, prednisone, Immuran, amphogel, Mycitracin. (There was a boy at Tulane that kept one seventeen years.) (Tides are an enigma in the islands.) (Exercise caution in anchoring and navigating.) (Water is precious on the ocean.)

Good ideas. The shortwave radio. The Children's Hour. How to tune in to it? The flags, the telltales, diving the wreck, available light, the Nikonos. As I suspected it is always the killed who object to killing. Bully Beef for lunch. Stupid. Dumb. Stupid. Dumb. Why'd I do that? What about lettuce? Water? Bacteria in water? Am I the killed or killing?

'They'll leave us when we turn back in at Jost Van Dyke,' Li said. 'They don't go in the channel any more. I haven't seen one inside the channel in years.'

'Can we eat at Foxy's tonight?' Jimmy asked.

'*Everything is wind on a sailboat*,' Sally said. 'How does that sound for the title of a chapter?'

'If Sally wants to,' Li said. 'I heard Foxy built a new swing on the tree where he sells shirts. Some kind of mechanical swing. You get a free swing if you buy a shirt. I've been wanting to see it.'

'I don't care what we do,' Sally said. 'As long as we get to a hardware store tomorrow morning. Are you sure they'll have what we need on Virgin Gorda?'

'If they don't have it there it won't be anywhere in the islands closer than Saint John's.'

'Well, we have to get clippers,' Sally said.

'Not clippers. Bolt cutters. If they don't have any at the store we'll get some from Little Dix. I know a guy at Little Dix that'll get one for us.'

'We've got all the diving stuff,' Jimmy said. 'There're two tanks.'

'Well, don't go getting any ideas about diving,' Sally said. 'I'm the only one that's going diving.'

'I know how,' he said. 'I've done it in the pool a hundred times. I can do it as well as you can.'

'Well, you aren't going to do it. Besides, I need you in the dinghy. I need you to stay on top and let the light down. It isn't going to take very long, you know. It's really a simple thing to do.'

'Then why hasn't anyone ever done it?' he said.

'I don't know,' Sally said. 'Maybe because they aren't from Georgia.'

They sailed in peace for a while. Li untied the wheel and they headed back into the channel to moor for the night at Trellis Bay. 'We know nothing,' she said, looking at Sally, who had pulled up a cushion beside her.

'We know how to make this boat,' Jimmy said. 'We know how to sail it.'

'He's got you,' Sally said.

'You have a criminal mind,' Li said. 'You will grow up to be a banker.'

'Go put some wine on ice,' Sally said. 'We'll celebrate.'

'You aren't supposed to drink. Uncle Malcolm said you weren't supposed to drink.'

'It doesn't hurt me,' Sally said. 'Unless he's watching. Actually it's very good for me.'

'He said it wasn't good for you.'

'Nothing is good for me,' she said. 'Therefore I am free to do anything. Come on, Jimmy. Put some wine in the cooler for your old aunt. And get on the radio and make reservations at Foxy's or there won't be any lobster left. And for God's sake, everyone remember to wear socks. There're sand fleas all over the beach at Foxy's. The last time I was there I got eaten alive. I sat up all night putting gin on my legs.'

She's going to get drunk, Li decided. Well, it never takes her long. I'll give it two hours from the time she opens the wine till she passes out.

It took three and a half hours. First there was a bottle of wine on the boat. Then a long diatribe against Republicans on the dinghy ride to Foxy's. Then she bought T-shirts for everyone in Guntersville. Then she bought a conch shell and some coral earrings. Then another bottle of wine. Then the dance.

Just about the time the lobster was put on the table Foxy put a record by Aretha Franklin on the record player. By the third bar of music Sally was out on the dance floor. Foxy's wife, Dreamy Malone, had danced with Sally before. She came out from behind the bar. The two women faced each other across eighteen feet of sand-covered pavement. Sally did her fabulous half-backbend. Dreamy countered with a bump and grind and they met in the middle with their arms in the air. 'Oh, you don't call anymore,' Aretha was singing. 'I sit alone and sigh.' 'I'm gonna knock on your door. Tap on your windowpane.' Sally did some steps from an old tap routine. Dreamy countered with a series of pirouettes. Then they really got down to it. Their hands met and parted. They were back to back. Then in each other's arms. 'I'm gonna knock on your door.

*Tap on your windowpane. Till you come back again. That's all I'm
gonna do.'*

By the time the record was finished everyone in the bar was
on their feet applauding. Dreamy helped Sally back to her
seat. Sally bowed to the audience, took a few bites of her
lobster and passed out with her head on Jimmy's lap.

'I'm glad Uncle Malcolm isn't here,' he said.

'So am I,' Li Moon agreed.

Jimmy was awake before dawn. Sitting on the prow eating a
sandwich, washing it down with ginger ale. The boat was
anchored in a wide harbour off Trellis Bay. The sea was calm,
the flags and telltales barely moving, the dinghy knocking
against the prow.

In a distant valley a shack leaned into the hill, a white shack
with a red roof. A woman came out the door and walked
down to the beach. She leaned over and began to wash a pan
out in the ocean. Jimmy could see her breasts moving as she
scoured the pan with sand. He stuffed the rest of the sandwich
in his mouth and turned his eyes away.

Farther along the shore were a few small houses, a white
church with brown shutters and a grey British customs house
with a pier for dinghies.

The hatch cover opened and Sally stuck her head out. 'Tie
that dinghy down, will you?' she said. 'I feel horrible. Jesus
Christ, I feel bad.'

'Remember that Christmas we came down here and they
came out and serenaded us with Christmas songs?' he said. 'I
think this is where we were. I think it was this island.'

'It was the Grenadines,' Sally said. 'Don't you remember?
Where we saw the whales. Come on, Jimmy, do something
with that dinghy. It's driving me crazy.'

She disappeared back down into the cabin making loud

theatrical groans. Jimmy went back to the stern and tied down the dinghy. Two black boys appeared on the beach. They walked down the pier and put their gear into a fishing boat. A cow called from somewhere in the village. The boat took off across the water, the sun broke from above the mountains, a voice was singing in a cabin.

Mustique, he decided. That's the name of it. Where the English princess lives. That's where they sang to us. He was looking up into the rigging, remembering his mother saying the princess liked young boys. He wondered if she would like him. She might hear about him setting the sharks free. She might read about it in the papers. He imagined his picture in the paper and the princess seeing it. Bring that boy over here to me, she would say. I like the way that boy looks. That's the boy that turned the fish loose.

This time tomorrow they'll be free. They'll be swimming off any place they want to go. He imagined them in a pack, sea turtles and sharks and angel fish and fat little puffer fish all swimming along like an armada, headed for the open sea.

'We're leaving as soon as we get ready,' Li Moon said. She had walked up so quietly he hadn't heard her. 'Do you want breakfast before we go?'

'I already had a sandwich. Is she OK?'

'She's OK. She's getting up. She's just excited.'

'She almost did it last year. If Uncle Malcolm hadn't gotten the toolbox away from her. She was drunk and he knocked her down on the deck and got it away from her. Then it fell overboard. Uncle Malcolm had to dive for it the next morning. But we still had to pay for some of the tools. He was just trying to keep her from hurting herself.'

'We'll do it this time. I can feel it.'

'Don't let her get drunk again, OK? Don't let her drink wine.'

'That isn't up to me. Or to you.'

They looked at each other. Li Moon removed all the expression from her face. Jimmy removed all the expression from his. They almost bowed.

'I could make a sailor out of you,' she said.

'All right,' Sally yelled from the cabin. 'Somebody get ready to lifeguard me. Here I come.' She was coming up the hatch wrapped in a towel. She stepped over the lifeline, did a lovely clean dive into the water and swam off into the morning sun. By the time she pulled herself back up on the motor the boat was ready to sail.

'Let's hit it,' Li said. 'We've got a long day ahead of us.'

They sailed out around the southern tip of the island and started toward Virgin Gorda. Li was in a hurry now. She moved from tiller to mainsail to ginny not saying a word, making small precise adjustments to the sails and rudder, not asking for any help, not wanting any.

'What are we going to do?' Jimmy said. 'Tell me exactly what we're going to do.'

'We'll go in the dinghy sometime in the morning, oh, about three or four. Then you can let the light down in the water while I go down with a tank and cut it open. I looked at it for a long time last year. There's nothing to it. A baby could do it. There are these posts, uprights, about ten feet apart and all I have to do is cut an opening. Then I'll get back in the dinghy and we'll watch them swim away. Li will stay on the *Wind Chime*.'

'You ought to throw the clippers away after you use them. So they won't have any evidence.'

'Do you think they'll get my fingerprints and track me down?'

'No, but they might find out and fire Li Moon.'

'That's why she's staying on the *Wind Chime*.'

'No, it isn't,' Li said. 'The reason I'm not going is because I can't swim. And I don't care if they fire me. One more cruise with a couple of rotten spoiled lawyers' wives and I'll end up in jail for murder. The one before you got here was the end. This whining girl from New Orleans who cried every morning. I'm not kidding you. She cried. They're getting worse, and there're too many boats. They don't know what they're doing. They can kill you.'

'You could come and live in Guntersville,' Jimmy said. 'We would like to have you there.'

The ship's chandler's store on Virgin Gorda had what they needed. A pair of wire cutters the British proprietor promised would cut through anything. 'You don't need bolt cutters. This is a nice little tool, actually. Look at these jaws.' He ran his finger along the cutting edge. 'What do you need it for?'

'To cut a chain-link fence?' Sally said.

'Well, be damned careful when you do. That wire's going to pop when you cut it. They string those things tight. It'll pop on you if you're not watching.'

'Thank you,' Sally said. She took the cutters in her hand. She slipped them into her bag and paid the man.

They sailed through the pass between Gorda Sound and Mosquito Bay with all sails flying, Jimmy at the helm, Sally tending the lines, and Li Moon sitting on the hatch cover filing her fingernails.

'Aren't you even going to watch the sandbars for me?' he said.

'You know the way,' she said. 'You went through here last week.'

'Well, at least tell me what to do,' he said.

'What if you were alone? What would you do if no one was with you?'

'I'd motor through,' he said.

Sally giggled. 'Loosen the ginny,' he said. 'Let out on the ginny. Hurry up.'

'I'm doing it as fast as I can,' she said. 'You should have told me sooner.'

They went in to dinner at The Bitter End, tying the dinghy up to the pier with the other boats, walking around the edge of the pen, pretending to admire the fish, feeling tight and conspiratorial.

It was a hot afternoon, hot and still. The fish looked colourless and apathetic. Hardly worth saving, Sally said to herself.

'They look terrible,' Jimmy said. 'They look all washed out.'

'It's the weather,' Li said. 'And oil from the boats. It gets on their fins.'

'That makes me want to throw up,' Sally said.

'Well, don't do it now,' Li said, looking around to see if anyone was listening. 'Come on. Let's go in and order dinner.'

They sat at a wicker table in the bar drinking lemonade and pretending to talk about other things, taking turns getting up and wandering around the resort asking questions of everyone they saw.

It was still light in the sky when they finished dinner and started back out to the sailboat.

'I can't wait much longer,' Sally said. 'I can't stand it.'

'Think about them,' Jimmy said. 'Think about swimming around that pen for a whole year.'

'Some of them have been there longer than that,' Li said. 'The turtles don't even bother to die.'

They woke at three and began to stir around the galley. 'Let's do it now,' Sally said. 'There's no reason to wait any longer.' She pulled on a bathing suit. She spit into her mask, filled it with tap water and washed it out. She adjusted the snorkel for the fourteenth time. She got out the clippers and cut the edge of a cookie sheet with them. 'They work,' she said. 'They really work.'

'I want you to promise to be careful,' Li said. 'There's no reason to get caught.'

'There's nothing to it,' Sally said. 'I've been diving in caves, Li. Remember that. I went night diving in the caves at Roatan. This is nothing compared to that.'

'Nothing is nothing in the ocean,' Li said.

'Where's my weight belt?' Sally said. 'I had it a minute ago. Oh, damn, what did I do with it?'

'Here it is,' Jimmy said. 'I was wearing it for you. Why did you put so much on it?'

'It's only three pounds. I need that much to stay down. Well, that's everything then. Are the tanks in the dinghy?'

'Everything's there. I checked everything four times. Quit asking me if everything's there. Come on, let's go.'

They walked from the galley to the back of the boat. Jimmy first, Sally behind him and Li Moon bringing up the rear. The moon was huge and white, far to the east in a starry sky. Their shadows lay across the boat, mixed in with the shadows of the lines and rigging.

'What will they think?' Jimmy said. 'When they get out?'

'They won't think anything,' Sally said. 'They'll just start swimming.'

Li sat on the hatch cover watching their progress across the water. She touched her sleeves with her fingers, concentrating on the little boat as if she could blow them to shore.

Let her turn the fish loose if she must. Let her believe anything she

wishes. It is all a dream. The 10,000 things we desire and dream of.
Who am I to tell her that in the morning they will all come swimming
back to where they were fed.

'If you're getting tired,' Sally said, 'I'll row.'

'I'm not tired. Besides, we're almost there. Going back we'll use the motor.'

'Be real quiet when we get to the pier. Don't knock against it with the boat.'

'You catch it. You're in front.'

'You're sure they're only nurse sharks?'

'Well, I asked everybody in the place. Besides, they're so fat they wouldn't eat you in a million years. Look, Sally, do you want me to do it?'

'No, I don't want you to do it. What if they won't swim out?'

'What do you mean?'

'I mean, after we cut it, what if they won't go out?'

'Let them worry about that. Look, you want a cookie? I brought some with me.'

'I want a drink,' she said. 'Hand me that bottle under the seat, will you?'

Aboard the *Wind Chime* Li Moon kept watch. The halyard tapped twice against the mast, then tapped again. Li swore to herself in Chinese and in French. Like all good sailors she was annoyed by the sound of anything loose on a boat. She got up and tied it down. When she resumed her posture the dinghy had made it to the pier.

'Be quiet,' Sally said.

'I'm being quiet. You're the one that's talking.'

'Here, do this for me.' She squirmed around on the seat and leaned forward so he could strap the tank on. She tested the gauges and put the mouthpiece into her mouth. Sally hated diving equipment. It was too heavy, too cumbersome, always in the way. She had been a swimmer at the school she went to in Virginia. Her specialty had been the butterfly. She moved her arms in a circle, feeling the constriction of the straps, remembering that small hot indoor pool, steam rising, clouding the windows, pulling on her cap, bending her knees, dying to win.

'Have you got the lights?' she said. 'Are you sure they work?'

'They work.'

'Check them again.'

He flipped the switches on the underwater lights, holding them down into the water. Several small fish came swimming up as soon as the light came on.

'They work.'

'The minute one of them goes out start blinking the other one. I might not even know which way is up.'

'I know.' He attached one of the lights to the weighted line so he could let it down beside her as she descended. The other one hung from the back of the dinghy as a marker.

'I still think you ought to work from the bottom up,' he said.

'Are you kidding? I'm not going to cut the whole thing anyway. I'm just going down about six feet. If they're too dumb to swim out of that they can just stay in the cage.'

'You ready?'

'I think so.'

'Then go on. Unless you want me to do it.'

'You watch those lights.' She held her nose and tumbled backwards into the ocean. In a moment she came up beside him holding the side of the boat.

'I forgot the fucking weight belt. Give it here.'

He took it off and handed it to her. 'Don't drop it,' he said. 'Be careful not to drop it.'

She adjusted the weight belt, stuck the regulator back in her mouth and reached for the light.

'All right,' she said. 'Keep hold of that line and don't let it get ahead of me. Pay attention, Jimmy. You watch me like a hawk.'

'I'll do it,' he said. 'I'll do it if you're scared to do it.'

She moved down into the water without answering him. She could see fairly well. She studied the post for a moment. The fence was attached to the post in a professional manner, as such things go in the islands. She pulled out the clippers and cut through the first strand, supporting her right hand with her left hand. She could feel the sound as the clippers cut into the metal. The wire snapped apart like a bone.

Several fish swam up to the edge of the pen. Behind them the shapes of the sharks and turtles moved in her imagination. She cut another strand. Then two more. Then three. Something moved beside her in the water. She backed away from the post. It was a turtle swimming by, coming to see about the light.

Oh, shit, she thought. They're going to eat me up. She moved back to the fence and cut another strand. Well, I can't quit. Jimmy would tell everyone in Guntersville if I did. He'd never be able to keep his mouth shut.

She was breathing heavily now, making a rasping sound against the mouthpiece. Maybe I'll use up all the air. Then I'll have to stop. She clenched her teeth down on the regulator and cut a few more pieces. Well, I have to do it. Goddammit, I am going to do it if it's the last thing I ever do in my life.

She went back to work in earnest, cutting steadily for a few minutes, moving down the post until she was almost four feet underwater. The light moved steadily along beside her. On the other side of the pen the shapes of the fish moved along as she moved. She began to worry that they would be cut on the jagged edges of the wire when they made their escape.

She managed to move down another six inches before the sight of a pair of eyes that seemed an inch wide made her completely lose her nerve. She surfaced, gasping, and pulled herself up on the edge of the boat. Jimmy took hold of her arms.

'What's wrong? What's going on? Are you done?'

'I'm scared to death. That's what's going on. I'm afraid one of them will get cut and they'll start a frenzy.'

'They're only nurse sharks.'

'I don't care. There's something spooky in there.'

'Let me do it. I can do it. I've done it in the pool a million times. Come on. Let me finish doing it.'

'Look, Jimmy, reach in that bag and get that gin and pour me some, will you?'

He did as he was told. He handed the cup to her and she drank it like water. 'OK,' she said. 'Now I'm going to finish it.'

'How far down does it go?'

'I can't tell.'

'How far are you going to cut it?'

'Not much farther. As far as I think it needs to go.' The gin arrived at her brain. *Silver bullets*, she thought. *Who called it that?* She descended again and went back to work. The eyes were still following her but now she didn't care. The fence only went down a few more feet. Below that was cheap wire mesh. *What a makeshift job. Just like a bunch of college boys. Well, I may as well go on and cut it all the way while I'm here*. She took three or four breaths of the air. It was so cool, a distillation of air. *A few more feet. Than I can brag about this till the day I die*.

She cut the last strand of wire. *Fini*, she thought. The section of wire slammed her through the water. Rolled and pushed and shoved her through the water, tore the regulator from her mouth. She breathed in water. Then it was only water. She had always known it would be water.

Jimmy was standing in the dinghy screaming. Aboard the boat Li Moon saw men come running out of the buildings. Lights came on. The body was lifted on to the pier. Li climbed up on the deck beside the mast and stood there in the moonlight, not even weeping, not able to shed a tear. It was completed. It was done.